OGRE

Brian G. Berry

ISBN-13: 9798839926097
ISBN-10: 1477123456

Cover design by: jorgeiracheta
Library of Congress Control Number: 2018675309
Printed in the United States of America

To Damien Casey, I couldn't get the formatting corrected, so I reverted to the standard :
(I thank you for your help, and make sure to send me pickles next time with your books.

"Why, you don't believe in Squatch?"

"Hell no."

"Then why the hell did you come?"

"Because I like to kill shit."

-Interaction, Abominable (2006)

CONTENTS

PREFACE

Quick Note:

The story ahead is a fast paced, gore drenched slaughter. If you are in the mood for pages dipped in red then you're in the right spot. I wrote this in place of an anthology I had planned to release this year. Originally I intended to have a sequel to my "Campfire Tales Beneath a Pallid Moon" but scrubbed the idea and instead penned this short novella. I've done my utmost to deliver a piece that is straight forward and wastes little time. I appreciate you and thank you for buying and reading and supporting me. Now, enjoy the woods!

CHAPTER 1

June, 1987
11:35pm

It was a silent night. Unusually so. Each night he was greeted with the sounds of the woods and its nocturnal emergence. The sounds of critters foraging in the bush, scampering across pine needles and disturbing branches and brush, picking at things in his rain gutters and scratching along his roof. Bats, too, were a common sight when the sun went cold. Across the face of the moon their wings beat and their squeals pierced the night in search of the massing clouds of insects that sheeted the surface of river arteries, bogs, lakes, and feeding troughs and such. But all that commotion was strangely absent on this particularly silent night.

Crawford Miller pulled deep on his pipe, an ember burning bright in the bowl, throwing a tangerine glow up his face. A man of many years; the lines on his brow, etched beneath his eyes, curled around his lips, up his neck, those lines told tales. His eyes, two points of blue iron that never wavered in the face of hardship, looked out on the broad clearing that lay past his porch. A pinch over seven decades, he was a man who took pride in his ability to retain luster in his property where others seemed to allow nature to reacquire its unrelenting reach.

Blowing a cloud yonder, Crawford examined with a keen pupil the land beyond his porch. A land of congested pine clusters, spruce, and fir, hemlock and brush, all of which enclosed his lot with a wall of spiky, blooming green and stunted clumps, only wedged open for grazing by his hand so many long years before.

Looking on the sky, one could never truly appreciate the moon that looked out over this land unless they had the blessing of the Lord to sit beneath this sky and gander at its dominance. It hung above his home, a bone white disk amidst a sable ocean of pearls. Its silver lambency carved aside the shadows from the meadow where they sat like black walls in the woods.

"Sure is a quiet one," he said to nobody but himself.

Unlike earlier that night when the earth seemed to shift its weight around, shake the mountains that reared up to bite the stars with their tapering rocky points. Seventy years breathing on this land and he could never recall one of those years that the earth shook itself with such violence.

"Must be getting old," he told the earth, pulling off his pipe. "Sitting in the same spot for so long,

I suppose you have to wring out the kinks every now and again."

But it was more than just the earth turning itself over and shaking loose the pictures from his walls, rattling curios from his cabinets, but of that strange, flickering band of lights that struck the mountain with such force it made him question his own eyes, and mind. Much like lightning, but something about it looked … *artificial.*

Disturbing his ruminations, a sound picked at his ears as he drew a mouthful of smoke. It was a rustling sound just beyond the clearing where the moon failed to manifest shape. Narrowing his eyes, Crawford could swear he'd seen something peculiar shaking them great big pines. Stoic, he pulled his pipe, wondering about such things as bears and night cats, predatory things that were liable to take a bite out of his three steeds just past sight.

Engrossed as he was, he retired such ruminations as something screamed, loud and frightening. It was the sound of an animal in piteous agony. A loud and screeching sort of sound that put a man to shivers and made him question just what in the hell he'd heard.

Crawford unplugged his pipe from his mouth, stared out in those black woods flushed with shadow.

His heart beat something unpleasant in his chest.

His breathing came in short bursts. He felt

funny; thought about backing up and grabbing the phone, ringing sheriff Caudel, let him know that he heard some screaming out in the woods. But ultimately he repealed that notion; decided to ash his pipe, head back inside his home for something else.

Black flooded his home like a funereal shroud. Above the cobblestone hearth sat enough firepower to fell an enraged grizzly. Crawford took it in his hands, broke open the breach, slotted two shells and started back for the door.

Dorothy shuffled downstairs, came around the corner in that floral nightgown she'd been wearing going on thirty years, her curly silver locks bound back with a length of purple fabric.

"For the love of Christ, honey," she whispered. "What was that awful sound outside?"

"Not certain sweetheart, but I think it came from the horses."

"Coyote's again?" she asked timidly, arms folded across her bosom in shudder.

"I reckon." Crawford grabbed an oil lantern, struck a match and put a flame in its center. "I'm headin' outside to check on things. Stay by the phone and keep Brutus indoors until I call for you to release him."

Brutus—an old bloodhound—came sauntering up on weak legs—legs old and brittle as those of his owners.

"Sweetheart don't go out there, could be wolves or grizzly this time," Dorothy snapped in a voice made weak with fear.

Crawford tapped the iron barrels of his coach gun. "I ain't worried none. I just hope whatever caused that scream decided it ain't worth the trouble—keep close to the phone."

Back on the porch, Crawford held the gun low, the lantern up and throwing weird and stranger shadows in his path. His slippers crunched a carpet of scattered needles across the clearing; the eye of the moon followed his lank figure, leaning a shadow of him that seemed to lengthen and shiver in the low brush; growing obscene in the wall of dense pine out beside his gravel drive. Pushing its flaming globe out ahead of him, Crawford caught a glimmer of something near where the horses ought to be resting.

"Something damn funny is goin' on around these parts," he said, curious about the absence of his steeds.

Cautious, Crawford stepped forward, a bulk of glistening mounds were at odds with his sight. It looked like something wet and stacked in segmented piles.

A few more steps forward edged the scene with his lantern light.

Crawford gasped, stifling a moan in his chest.

"For the love of Peter—"

The light played tricks. Spokes of firelight painted a grisly scene. Crawford was at a loss of a particular vocabulary. "I—by God—what—"

It was appalling. Three horses, or what remained of such beasts, were ghastly mounds of blood and scattered wet things, marinating in pools of red. The heads were missing, like something tore 'em off with a shearing tool. Their bellies were opened up, bursting with meat and loops of what looked hideously like balls of big red worms uncoiling from themselves. From right to left, it was a massacre. So much blood and coils of foul smelling things.

He called a warning over his shoulder, his voice scratchy and loud. "Dorothy, I—"

Crawford froze as one might caught in the paralysis of fear. No, not fear, but an enveloping terror that wrapped about his mind like a copperhead aiming to polish his skull. The lantern came up, the gun rising with the expectancy of some lumbering forest creature painted with a red mouth, fangs out to here and big black eyes that looked on a man as another slab of raw meat to fill its belly.

Crawford swallowed.

"Something in those trees," he whispered to himself.

Crawford started backward. Careful not to fall, he kept his gun on those woods, his eyes darting to anything not hit with the sudden breeze that swept along the pines.

He choked on a gasp as a towering bulk brushed along the pines that loomed to the stars in great black spires.

His heels shuffled back with more haste, back toward his home.

Dorothy was shouting about something, but none of what she said had reached his ears. Keeping his face to the woods, he worked himself back, when something caught and widened his eyes. And whatever it was had put an icicle up his spine. A bellowing blow of his shotgun broke the brooding silence of the woods. Pellets rattled the wall of conifers, yet no sound returned but the whispering breeze.

Crawford dropped the lantern, put his back to the dead horses and woods and loped with an old man's gait back to the safety of his stead.

"Hun, what's wrong—what did you see out there?"

Crawford heaved with old lungs, closing the door behind him, beads of sweat on his ashen face. "I dunno' darlin', something unspeakable. It was *big*. The horses—" he shook his head "—ain't nothin' left."

Dorothy shivered, yelped out something in her throat.

"Get Caudel on the line, tell him to bring some guns up to the ranch, something big is in these woods—"

As to confirm such fears, something brushed up against their home, and they knew it not to be the hedge below the windows shaken by the breeze.

Dorothy and Crawford went silent. Their ears open, old hearts slamming against feeble bones.

"What was that?" Dorothy whispered so low Crawford thought maybe his own mind was speaking to him.

Another brush, this time along the front door, and with it the sound of heavy breathing around the seals. It brought an emptiness to their lungs.

Brutus started growling with that big brown muzzle of his. Moonlight spoked through drapes limned his cataracts a sharp silver.

Crawford stared off at the door, jaw slacked open, gun trembling in his hands.

"What is it?" Dorothy asked again.

Crawford shook his head. "Whatever it is, it's big. *Real* big. The horses—" he cut himself off again, thinking it better not to describe just what sort of thing he'd seen out yonder in those woods, if only to keep sanity in check.

Brutus started barking, his muzzle snapping, spittle flecking around his head, his fur rigid.

"Wolves? Is it wolves?"

"Don't think so, dear, this is something bigger than any wolf—yammer down, Brutus."

A shadow crossed the picture window in the family room. A big and amorphous sort of shadow that put their minds working to cogitate phantoms unholy to this plane. But it was the amplified profile of a claw which prevented any mention of things natural to these woods.

"What was *that?*" Dorothy pointed with a shaking finger.

Again, Crawford shook his head, replaced a fresh shell with the empty.

Glass broke in the kitchen.

Dorothy screamed.

Crawford swung his gun on the corridor leading to the kitchen.

Silence reigned as ears opened. Even Brutus decided it prudent enough to shutter that muzzle of his.

Crawford took hesitant steps towards the kitchen, Dorothy breathing down his back, the tips of her fingers digging into his waist.

"Keep quiet, honey," he told her, not daring to take his eyes from above the shotgun.

Swinging into the kitchen, moonlight hit the fragments of scattered glass like silver chips on the tiles. Crawford looked to the window, saw the drapes exhaling with gusts.

"Smell that?" he asked.

Dorothy shivered. "It's awful, what is it?"

Crawford's nose twitched. "Smells like blood, and a lot of it."

Brutus started barking at the front door.

Crawford and Dorothy swung back as one, eyes on the black hall, ears ringing from the barking, nerves pinching, hearts failing.

Hurrying down the hall, reaching the family room, they looked on Brutus just as the door was suddenly blown wide open with a gust—or what they thought could be a gust. Brutus shot forward, a dark flash of snapping jaws that barked his way out the door.

"BRUTUS!" Crawford shouted over the gun.

Dorothy screamed.

Not a foot away from reaching the door, they both shuddered at the sound of a dog wailing in death somewhere in the shadows beyond the porch.

Dorothy instinctively started forward, leaving the shelter of her home, screams rising shrill from her throat. "*Brutus!*"

Crawford reached out a shaking hand for his wife, but it was too late. "Dorothy, get back here!"

Scarce a sliver past the porch of their home, something like the trunk of a massive serpent, hairy as a grizzlies leg, reached down and with a revolting hand not dissimilar to that of an ape, fingers matted with fur and tapered with grisly black hooks, scooped up the frail old woman by the gray curls, lifting her out of sight with a heart breaking scream in her throat.

Crawford swooned in the frame of the door.

Dorothy's screams quickly dissolved into blood curdling cries that shook the walls of his mind until her anguish was cut silent by a bubbling throttle in her throat. Blood flooded the gutter, surging over the edge like rainwater. Two slabs of something meaty rolled off the roof, striking the ground with a wet spatter.

Crawford, consumed by the imbalance of a

black terror, stared at the two ragged halves of his wife whose entrails pushed from twin cavities amidst a rising tide of blood.

Subjugated by a molten rage, he cried out in his throat, eyes rounded in his skull, charging from his home. Turning, he threw the barrels up into the starlight and saw something perched on his roof, silvered by the moon. Something colossal and black and heaving with misted breath—something alien and awful and hideous to a mind on the precipice of lunacy. Two points of red light lit up in that squat broad head. Crawford shouted and gave that abomination two barrels before its bulk leaped from the roof with an inhuman scream trailing from its mouth, absorbing Crawford beneath a fan of thrashing black claws which quartered his frail body down into a hideous and scattered slop.

CHAPTER 2

Brittney Gatten stared out the window, sunlight in her face. It was country she was well accustomed to, something she craved and loved waking up to. The sound of nature rising to the early morning dawn of a peaking sun cresting a broken and blue ridge, spoking amber into a valley of dark pines. It was special; an experience only reflected by those who have shared in the moment of such imagery. Mornings like this were to be captured not with a camera, but the eye.

Out the window, opened to her eyes, was a vast league of green spikes and bristles that seemed to stretch endlessly to a rosy band of sky. Feeling the rise of elevation inclining below the bus, the open valley was suddenly blotted out by a wall of coarse timber and brush that darkened the interior, lightly broken only by the lancing of amber, moted by the dust of the road.

Seated around her were the faces of counselors she would be spending the next six weeks alongside. Six in total; three of which were women, and the other half were men. She met each briefly as she boarded the bus, but shared nothing but quick observations and pleasantries. Like herself, some were in their own head, staring out the window or idly chatting amongst each other. One of the guys, Marcus, a monster of muscle and ego, was staring into a hand mirror, picking diligently at the black curls of his hair which sat atop his head like a bow on a present. Seated two rows behind her was a younger woman like herself, name of Julie, with short brown hair curled inward to her neck. She was reading aloud from a paperback, and from the descriptions of the words, Brittney wondered if maybe she were studying up on poison plants and edibles and things of that nature—things they would likely come across during nature walks and overnights in the woods.

The others were gathered around the driver, picking his brain about the area; about the camp, which none of them had seen so far; only heard fleeting things about from the owner over the phone.

She was looking forward to this ever since last summer when she learned there was an opening for prospective counselors at a newly developing summer camp taking shape in a rugged, mountainous enclave in the more north-western region of Washington state—a place only several hours from her home further down near the Oregon border. Camp Starlight it was called, supposedly named after the lambent star fields that filled the night sky above the camp.

A camper of many summer camps during her younger years as a child, she was happy to jump on the opportunity. At twenty-three, she felt a bit too old when she applied, but after a lengthly conversation with the owner, a nice man by the name of Pete, he assured her she would likely be the youngest one of his counselors on the roster. That made her smile. But then she started thinking if she were *too* young for the job.

It was the sound of pine needles and gravel crunching under tread that brought her out of her wandering mind. The brakes of the bus hissed, a swish of the doors fell back on their track. The driver raised himself out of his seat.

"Okay counselors, we're here!"

After they filed out, the group was assailed with the scent of pine resin on the wind—a cool wind that blew off the shimmering blue surface of the lake. Bags shouldered, the group stood around loosely, chattering softly, peaking around at the facilities, shaded by the ceiling of bushy green needles above.

Brittney let her eyes wander and inspect the grounds. Compared to the camps she frequented in her youth, this place had few facilities she could count, and most of what she saw was minimal in expanse, and lacking an ethic of coherent craftsmanship.

She counted six cabins, all wrapped in a dark

wood siding with white trim capped with snow retention roofing dusted with pine needles. She spotted a baseball diamond that sat a distance back from the cabins in a wide clearing—she noticed the grass blades were thick and bushy and untrimmed, the fence enclosing the lot was sagging and rattling lightly with the wind. She looked on the dining hall, or what she assumed would be the dining hall. A lodge that was squat and narrow and peaked and ugly, and she wondered exactly how many campers this place anticipated for the summer.

Drawing her attention away from the structure, her pupils caught sight of an *L* shaped maple deck extending out into the lake. Moored to its edge in a horizontal column, bobbing lightly with the sun glittering waves, were several canoes of walnut finish striped with yellow bands at the bow and stern. Aside from the beauty of the lake belted by a timber sea of green, sitting at the foot of a rocky pine flecked mountain, she'd seen better—*much* better.

"Place is a dump," Marcus said. "I mean, look at those cabins—and that dining lodge is a mess!"

"Does look a bit … unfinished," another counselor said, but whose name she had forgotten. Unlike Marcus, whose brutish body and muscle ridged limbs, this guy looked closer to her age and was slender and tall and blond. He was wearing a pair of tatter cuffed jean shorts and white shirt, a pack slung over his shoulder. "It is opening day, right?"

"Yeah," Julie said somewhat frustrated by the conditions. "I *think?*"

Marcus dropped his bag to the soil, his big arms folded over the twin iron shields of his broad chest. "Pete said this place would be ready when we arrived; looks like they just started painting the place."

Brittney looked to the dining lodge; to the cabins. "Where's the director?"

Five pairs of eyes were on her.

"Isn't there supposed to be a director?"

"No way darling," the unknown counselor said. "We're the only authority around here. Pete told me he might drop in during the summer at some point to check on things, but didn't say when or if he was certain."

"I've never worked at a camp without a director," another counselor said. "So, what's the next step—hey, where's the driver?"

The six of them looked around.

"He's probably inside taking a leak," Ron said. He was an older looking guy like Marcus, but where Marcus could press a boulder over his head with one arm, this guy had a frail sort of look to him that made Brittney wonder why he was even here. He was red haired and wiry and short.

"What about the cooking staff?" Brittney asked. "They don't expect us to cook, right?"

"Good question," the unknown counselor said. He stared off into the camp, scratching at his blond head.

"Pete said they would be arriving sometime this morning, so they should be here any time now," Marcus told them confidently. "In the meantime —" he grabbed his bag "—I'm checking on the cabins, then hitting the lake—I need a tan. Anybody with me? Jake? Ron?"

Jake! That was his name, Brittney thought to herself.

Jake started after Marcus. "Coming."

Ron went after the pair silently.

Brittney, Julie and: "What's your name again?" Brittney asked. "I'm terrible with names."

The black haired girl who looked around her age, maybe a year older said, "Angela."

"Ah, Angela—you two want to check out the cabins with me? See what we're in for this summer?"

The two nodded, heaving their bags and following after Brittney.

Typically shy in social matters, Brittney felt at ease in the woods. It was a special place for her; always had been. Something about the woods, maybe the wind and the smell of fresh pine; the un-poisoned air of a mountain climate, whatever it was, it did wonders for her self-esteem.

Even with the few discrepancies pointed out by her and the other counselors, the place had a rugged and isolated feel to it, so the conditions of the cabins and outbuildings being austere as they were, complimented its surroundings. It was much more different than the places she had been to in her youth, but something inside of her preferred it this way. It reminded her of camping with her own parents, back when they rejected standard campgrounds and forged the woods for those isolated pockets of paradise unknown to man. Places that took the effort of endurance and patience to reach. This place captured a piece of that: that solitude and detachment from the world, the possibility of adventure.

She smiled as the needles crunched underfoot and the wind blew through her blond hair. The smell of pine woods was a memory uncorked in her mind. She had a good feeling about this, and couldn't wait for the kids to arrive.

She just hoped the other counselors were just as excited as she was.

CHAPTER 3

Sheriff Roy Caudel was not altogether unfamiliar to the red tide wrought by rifles on the battlefield, or of injuries sustained during accidents in the mountains; even those poor souls opened in vital areas by the maw of some famished or hungry beast of the woods. And during his thirty years as the law around Starbright Springs, only one such hideous encounter looked much like what he was staring at right then, at the Miller's place.

Starbright Springs, a place of no vital repute to the world nor the map in any regard, just a patch of wooded paradise not fifty miles from the crashing breakers of the heaving Pacific. Enclosed in the heart of sky rearing conifers, it was spotted with lakes, riven with crashing rivers and split with the lucid threads of creeks; home to good and humble folk. And its latest addition—much to the chagrin of some of the people who populated its core—a summer camp.

Confident in his abilities over such a long period of enforcing the law to detect disparities between those of crime and those committed by the slavering jaw of some forest creature, he had an inkling that what he was looking upon was the work of something that started years before; something that combined the cunning of man and the relentlessness of a territorial primate. A memory he worked hard to bury away and disavowal its reality to maintain a sanity that was becoming more frail, induced by the awareness of such a foul and unholy abomination.

"Still can't put a finger on it sheriff," Deputy Clint Wilmont said.

Count yourself lucky to be uninformed of this horror, Caudel thought to himself.

"I remember last year—the grizzly attack up on Bald Ridge Trail? Thought I'd never see something so heinous like that again. Them poor folks ..."

Caudel nodded, his thumbs hooked inside the waistband of his olive trousers, his gun slack on his hip, the sun beating down on his back. The images of that hot summer evening of '86 flashed behind his eyes. It was a young couple, out on a hike, came across a wandering cub who lost its way, according to a witness who observed the two trailing the cub.

Momma bear—a big and hulking monster of fur and talons and teeth—got wind of her squealing cub, and let that couple know what sort of trouble they had found and ripped apart the hikers as if they were made of modeling clay. Blood lay in a thick congealed pool under the boiling sun.

Flies carpeted the gore; critters toiled the interiors, dragging out ropy wet things and mouthfuls of others. Carrion birds beaked apart the crowns, choking down knots of brain. Even the packs and gear which were scattered on the trail, were not spared the wrath of the claw. As horrible and mind bending as that scene was, it lacked the brutality of a malevolent and concerted mind; just the natural impulse and reciprocation of a pissed-off grizzly defending its young. But what his eyes showed him now, scattered at his boots, out in the grazing field, he'd seen enough to understand that what had taken place at the Miller's was by design, and a malevolent one.

"I recall the day," Caudel said blank faced.

Jeremy Burnett, Crawford Miller's neighbor, shuffled uneasily. "I just can't imagine something getting the drop on Crawford like this. The man was an experienced hunter; an excellent shot. Even his shotgun lying there beside him is empty. What sort of animal around here could do something like *this?*" It was the second time he inquired of that mystery, but this time vocally to the lawmen standing confused beside him and not in own his head. "Suppose it could be that grizzly again; even two shells fired at point blank ain't gonna' put the brakes on a monster like that."

It was Burnett who happened upon the ugly scene in the early afternoon rays of a torrid sun. Returning the pole pruner Crawford had loaned him the previous morning, Burnett about shit himself when he saw what was left of Dorothy baking in the heat; saw the pieces of Crawford searing like raw steaks on the gravel walk. He walked into the home a moment after he worked the contents of his belly up in a rose bush, rang the sheriff, told him of the horror out at the Miller place.

After Caudel and Wilmont arrived, they ran a quick grid of the land and discovered the hollowed out interiors of the horses—the three horses crusted with flies where their heads should have been instead of the grisly vacancy of such things. Not too far off the porch, they discovered Brutus, the old faithful bloodhound that followed Crawford around like a son. Like the horses, wasn't much remaining but his thick blue collar split in length with bits of flesh and hair smeared into the fabric; couple of bones thrust up out of a pile of scattered wet, red things.

You know what it was, don't you? Caudel thought to himself. *A secret so interred in that subconscious of your's that its reality has minimized over the years to nightmares and figments; you're forgetting old man, becoming rooted with fallacy …*

"You still think what did this is some sort of common animal do you?" Caudel snapped. "You happen to notice them horses out in the field? Looked like a goddamn broadsword butchered those beasts. Think something that walks on four legs had a helping in this?"

"What are you thinking, sheriff?" Wilmont

asked, curious as to why the sheriff sounded agitated with himself. In fact, Wilmont had a few suspicions regarding the sheriff ever since they stepped onto the property, like once he got a look at the remains, he seemed to be oppressed with a heavy burden of sorts that was out of character for him. It was strange to Wilmont that Caudel had not so much as gasped or said much of anything besides a few things mumbled from his lips that had no real meaning Wilmont could determine. The deputy himself had trouble keeping the abhorrence of the situation out of his mouth; fighting to keep his breakfast from packing up his throat.

Remaining silent, Caudel looked out across the clearing into the pines. His eyes wandered up the width of the mountains that loomed gaunt and precipitous over the property, to the vast, open blue sky. He thought about the strange bands of lightning that came together, lancing the sky a brilliant and odd color, licking those crags last night. Thought about the quake that had shaken the small town to its roots, fissuring forest roads, cracking a few homes open like yawning jaws.

It's starting again. It's returned...

It got him to thinking about that boy he found covered in blood so many long and paling years before.

It was only by a chance of luck he caught sight of the boy wandering aimlessly on a narrow forest road after a wrathful storm that blighted the area with flooding and heavy mud slides and pockets of lightning.

The boy—which he determined to be somewhere a year or two shy of an adult—had told him a wild yarn in fragmented English, something Caudel couldn't quite bring himself to understand or believe as his conditioning of civilization had made him skeptical of such tales relating to forest bogeys and monsters and ogres and such. A man of the woods his entire life, and not in one of those years of his childhood to that day could he ever recall seeing things of such nature. Of course, he'd suffered through his fair share of tales gathered around campfires, burped and exaggerated by drunken relatives and friends, none of which in their monstrous origins had bothered or interested him in the slightest.

Carefully winding their way down the mountain, headed back into town so Caudel could see to it that the boy receive aid for his wounds, the boy—whose name he never remembered on account it was a string of letters that escaped him over the years—related in no subtle terms that his family, a recessed survival of Duwamish, eking their life away from the federal reach, deep in the woods, had fell to the wrath of a demon. He related in hasty words and descriptions how he had escaped its claws but knew the demon would not relinquish in its pursuit until his blood and bones gorged its belly.

"*It came down with the storm,*" he told Caudel.

Conveyed to the earth by a great shaft of lightning, the horror from the stars had returned!"

Caudel pressed him for further information, but the boy just muttered on about the stars. "*It came from the stars, it came from the stars ...*"

Caudel thought the boy delirious, half naked as he was, speaking with the tongue of the uneducated, covered in blood that he couldn't logically explain. Besides a few lacerations that could have been the origin of stone ledges or limbs of tree and brush on the surface of his skin, nothing so minor could provide the sheet of red that clung to his body in a sticky coat. The prospect of a bear was foremost on Caudel's mind; maybe some lunatic; but a demon? It was laughable, and perhaps he would have chuckled a bit if it wasn't for those haunted glances staring blankly out of that blood spattered face.

He went on to further question the boy about this demon, but it was like picking the brain of the delusional.

It was at a sharp bend in the mud road that a splintered trunk of a pine tree blocked his route. Caudel told the boy he'd return once he figured a way around, much to the fear of the young man who explained to Caudel he could detect the presence of the demon in the woods nearby and shouted that the tree was a trap placed there by the demon. Caudel shrugged, unable to think of words to calm the boy's mounting terror that cracked his voice.

Fixing the boy with a smile, Caudel dismounted the cab. He sauntered over in the mud, scratched his head trying to come up with a solution to remove the heavy trunk aside, when a scream shattered his mind.

Nearly falling on his ass at the sound of that scream, Caudel swung back to face his rig, when he saw a hulking black shape steal off up into the woods, a boy kicking and screaming under one massive black arm like a flailing doll.

It took the color right out of his face seeing such an imposing shape with a frightened boy screaming the only way a frightened boy could scream. But it was only the beginning of—

"Sheriff? You okay," Wilmont asked after a silence seemed to imprison Caudel in thought.

Caudel looked to his deputy shaken out of his ruminations, then put his eyes back on the mountain again.

"You were saying you don't think this is the work of an animal?"

Another brief space of time picked at his mind before Caudel continued. "I don't know what to think about it." He stated flatly.

But in his mind, he was certain of things, things that if he admitted to his deputy and Burnett they'd think him off his mind again; think him too old for the position of sheriff. Nearly seven decades on this planet, thirty of which he spent working in the capacity of law for this town, he'd be damned if they or anyone think him incapable of his duty.

He looked down at the fly crawling mass of wet meat that belonged to Crawford Miller at his boots. "I'm not so quite sure that what we're dealing with here is … *natural*."

Wilmont looked lost. "Not *natural*, sir? You mean: not like an animal? You thinking somebody locally had a hand in this? Maybe an outsider? I did notice a few strange faces back in town recently."

Caudel spit something from his mouth, rubbed at his bristled chin. "I have my theories, deputy."

Wilmont stood there patiently, as if waiting for the sheriff to enlighten him of those theories. He wondered if maybe Caudel was having a lapse of reasoning, something he'd been wondering about the sheriff more and more of lately.

"Sheriff, I know it looks strange an all with this amount of … *damage* to the bodies, but, you do remember those poor hikers? What was left of 'em?"

Caudel nodded. "I remember it like it was only last week, son, but look here—" he pointed to something that had escaped notice of both Burnett and Wilmont "—that ain't no claw from a bear, nor any other animal sovereign to these woods."

Wilmont lowered himself, fingered the stub of a black hook-like thorn lodged between the pelvic wing of Dorothy's lower half. It took some effort, but he finally managed to pry it loose. His eyes roamed its surface in inspection. "The hell is so special about it? Looks no different from the claw fragment the grizzly left behind out near the hikers." He rolled it over in his hand. "Feels a bit heavier is all."

Burnett drew his cap off his head, swatted at the flies clouding the gap between the three of them, his eyes wandering over the arched, black, thorn-like nub. "What in God's name is that? A tooth? A fingernail?"

Caudel took the sickle shaped black hook from his deputy, ran a thumb over the back of its ebony surface. Grim images and speculations filled his mind, confirming that what he was looking at belonged to that black bodied monster he'd spied so many moons in the past. He looked to his deputy.

"Call Margaret, tell her to ring Cottman, let her know he'll need to clear out some space in the morgue. Also ring up Ranger Rundell, I'll need his assistance in shutting down the summer camp."

Burnett and Wilmont looked at one another, then onto Caudel. It was understandable to want to call for the camp's closure. Thinking of the children's safety was a priority when a dangerous animal was on the loose and harming individuals. But shutting down the camp wouldn't be as easy as the sheriff supposed it to be, even with the assistance of a federal ranger like Rundell. It was the first year of the camp's opening, he knew they would meet some heavy resistance from the owner who would frown at the warnings as pure bullshit, on account of the opposition the camp received from a handful of the population during its construction—say it was tactics to try and scare away business which in turn scares off parents, and their money.

But the inquiring glare in his eyes went beyond the sudden order of closure. Something about Caudel was throwing up red flags in his mind. He had a feeling the sheriff knew more than he was letting on. It was how he was supposed to get it out of him that would be an issue. Over the years, he learned that Caudel was a vault lacking a combination, so with that shelved in mind, he simply nodded, went for his radio.

"Yes, sheriff. I'll get right on it."

CHAPTER 4

It moved with the grace of a primate, one whose origin rested not in the cycle of recent ages, but of dim and forgotten recesses of time; from when the jungles ran deep with mystery and sired indescribable horrors that battled with the predecessors of man. A pendulum of might and madness, it swung amongst the pines, a black shadow of fur and claws and eyes that burned with molten evil.

Mercilessly its kind pounded and tore asunder the creatures of the woods, leaving behind ghastly mounds and smudges and traces of woodland critters; heads and arms and broken forms lay slashed in pools of blood.

During its descent from the stone peaks from which it received its wisdom and guidance and edicts, a cat of massive strength and weight contested with the beast. But the mountain cat soon learned an invaluable lesson, that the bulky monster of black was no common stranger invading its redoubt. It laid open the massive beige furred feline with the ease that the honed edge of an executioners sword cleaves a man's head from his shoulders.

At the foot of the mountain, the forest greeted the monster and even the wind seemed to freeze and frighten away. All was still but the eyes of the beast which roamed the timber ocean and the ears which opened and the claws that twitched and the massive breast that lifted with air.

It would reap a great slaughter, engorge its belly with the blood of the conquered; it would abscond with which was desired by the invader.

CHAPTER 5

After they left Cottman behind to deal with the bodies, or what was left of such things that could be considered traces of anatomy, sheriff Caudel and deputy Wilmont drove on in silence, headed up the hill to the ranger post.

During the drive, Caudel kept his eyes on the road, narrowing his gaze to the moted columns of sunlight which barred and obscured the path ahead. Even with both windows open, the air sucked into the cab was blowing hot and doing nothing to lessen the beads of sweat that clung to brow, bunched beneath arms, sopping chest and belly. Dust was pulled inside, clinging to the sweat, furthering their discomfort and unease.

But that was not what brought about irritable grunts and murmurings from Caudel behind the wheel. It was the terrible fact—the terrible knowledge—of that creature having returned.

"I gotta' ask," Wilmont injected. "What's going on sheriff?"

"What do you mean?"

"Don't play foolish with me, sheriff, I've known you long enough to understand when something is bothering you. So what is it? What's on your mind?"

Traversing a small bridge of uneven, rackety boards, sun limned both lawmen under a burning furnace, a rippling creek underway filled the cab with its sound. "It's nothing—nothing I want to discuss right now."

"If it's about the Miller's—"

"It's not about the goddamn Miller's!" Caudel snapped.

Wilmont looked on like he'd been slapped.

"Sorry, deputy. It's not about the Miller's—God rest their souls."

Wilmont discontinued his questioning. Maybe allowing Caudel a bit of breathing room would be better to help him work things out. Still, he was concerned. Concerned because after all these years of working in tandem with the sheriff, he had never seen him act so funny; so distant and aloof as he was acting right then. Maybe it was the years getting to him, maybe it was something else. Wilmont could never tell.

Driving on, they encountered a small group of hikers beneath the shade of some pines, shouldering gear, standing around a small bus of sorts that had been converted into what looked like a mobile camper.

Caudel slowed his pace, easing alongside the group.

"Howdy, you folks okay here?"

A tall, rangy looking man with big brown hair

in a pair of jean shorts and red plaid short sleeve, a heavy pack on his back, put a hand over his eyes to shield the sun. "Yes, sir, we're just preparing to head off, find a spot to camp."

Caudel looked at the camper, then back to the hikers. "In the woods?"

"Yes, sir."

"You have a permit?"

The man looked confused. "Permit?"

"For fires, son."

"Oh, I didn't think we needed a permit so long as we were careful, sir."

"You know how many people believe they're careful with fires in these woods?" Caudel asked him. "Every one of them. If you don't you have a permit, I'm afraid I can't allow you to make any fires in these woods."

A woman stepped forward, blond hair twisted into tails that hung down her shoulders, wide green eyes, a purple plaid short sleeve over a low-cut pink top. "Sheriff? Where do we get a permit?"

Caudel looked past the woman at the three other hikers who were no longer showing smiles.

"Up at the ranger station, he should be able to help you out."

"And where is the ranger station?" the tall guy asked.

Caudel pointed. "Follow this road, past the summer camp, and you'll see the station tucked back behind some trees. Keep an eye pealed for the sign. You can't miss it."

"Thank you, sheriff," the woman said.

"No problem, ma'am."

"And how much are one of these permits, sheriff?" tall man asked.

"Run you about five dollars, cash."

The hikers started for their pockets.

"If I may add one thing, I wouldn't recommend camping in these woods right now."

The hikers stared at the sheriff. The girl smiled. "Why is that sheriff?"

"Oh, been reports of a dangerous *animal* around these parts; hurt a few people further down the hill this morning; nasty business."

"Oh no, is it bad?" the girl asked.

"They're dead."

The girl stepped back like she swallowed something unpleasant, looking over her shoulder to her friends.

"I strongly suggest you four pack it up and head back home; come back another time when it's safer."

"Sir, we've had this planned for some time, we'll be careful, but we're not turning back—"

"You have shit in your ears boy? I said a goddamn animal killed two people today, and their steeds, and their goddamn dog! How much warning do you need?"

The man put his hands up, backed away to the group.

Caudel pointed a thick finger at him. "Now, instead of running that mouth of yours, why don't y'all save yourself any pain and pack it up now before you regret it."

"Yeah … thanks sheriff, we will."

Caudel eyed them all suspiciously. "Hate to come back down here and find pieces of you in the morning." He put the truck in gear and left the hikers behind in a cloud of dust and puzzled faces.

"Bit excessive sheriff?" Wilmont inquired.

"People have to know these woods are dangerous, deputy. Maybe I should have let them go into those woods ignorant of this animal, that what you think?"

"Not at all, I just … well—"

"Spit it out, Wilmont, I know you're itching to."

Wilmont sat in silence, staring over at Caudel, picking out the throbbing pulse in his temples, the sweat trailing down his cheeks, his eyes round and stressed.

"Well?" Caudel said.

"Nothing, sheriff."

"He's just trying to scare us is all."

"I don't know, Greg, I'm pretty scared thinking about a bear on the loose—"

"The sheriff never said it was a bear—look, are you coming with us or not?"

Charlotte bit her lip, looked to the eyes of her friends which were wide on her right then. "What do you think, Melissa?" she asked.

Melissa, brown hair bound back by a red

kerchief, a brown and tan plaid shirt, sleeves rolled up to her elbows, a white shirt beneath, shuffled uneasily. "I dunno—what if there *is* a bear on the loose you guys?"

Frank, a man with short black hair, blue shirt and gray khaki shorts, put his arm around her waist. "I got you baby, I won't let anything happen to you, I promise."

"Oh that makes me feel better, Frank—what are *you* going to do against a bear, huh?"

"I'm telling you guys there is no damn bear," Greg said bitterly. "That old sheriff is pulling our leg; he's just trying to scare us out of his woods. You see that look on his face?"

Charlotte nodded. "Yeah, I saw it—he looked genuine to me."

"Bullshit—he was feeding us a line of bullshit."

"Well, what about the people that were killed—was he lying about that too?"

Greg shrugged. "Maybe. I'm sure he was—now, are we all going camping? Or are we forgetting this whole thing and going home? Which, I would like to remind you, is two hours south from here."

The group mulled a moment.

Frank put his hand in the air. "I'm ready to camp, been waiting for this too long now to pack it up early."

Greg smiled. "See, Frank's with me. Now how about you two? Charlotte? Melissa?"

"Come on baby, remember what we planned to do?" Frank winked.

Melissa rolled her eyes. "Well … did you bring—did you bring the gun?"

Frank patted his hip. "Sure did. My daddy's .45."

"Well—"

"Come on babe, please?"

Melissa shrugged. "Okay."

Greg looked at Charlotte. "You coming?"

Sighing, she relented. "Fine, but I'm telling you now, if I see anything weird or hear anything funny—and that includes jokes—I'm out of there!"

"Fair enough."

Heaving their gear, securing their belts, the four soon merged beneath the weaving bows of the pine woods …

Caudel guided the truck along the narrow dirt path that wound in to the ranger station. Pulling into a pine needled spot, he silenced the engine, pocketed the keys and dismounted. Outside, the sun poured its heat onto him.

Wilmont came around the truck. "Think those kids will take you're advice, sheriff?"

"Knowing the young of today, likely not; suppose they're headed off into the woods now. Dumb fools."

Pushing into the ranger station, both lawmen were hit with a relieving cool wave. It felt good, eased away the sweat.

Inside, the place was laid out like one would expect when visiting a ranger station. Maps were pinned to the walls, filing cabinets lined in order —on top of which sat a stack of loose files and rotating metal fan trailing silver streamers. A couple of desks scattered with papers and writing material sat moted with sun spears beneath open windows, a radio counter, a cabinet of rifles and shotguns. Immediately through the door was a welcoming area for travelers and campers, a rack of brochures and trail maps, a drinking fountain with a stack of paper cups at its side.

Ranger Jim Rundell was seated behind his desk, his boots kicked up on the surface, leaning back in his chair with a paperback fanned open in his face. He looked over the pages at the visitors.

"Sheriff Caudel, good to see you, what can I do for you this fine afternoon?"

Caudel walked past the low swinging door dividing the room to the ranger office—which was the open room with two desks. "I'll be blunt: I need you're help in shutting down the summer camp."

"Starlight?"

"That's the one."

"I believe its opening day there today, sheriff—"

"Which is more the reason I need you're assistance in shutting it down immediately."

Rundell sat forward, slotted a bookmark, folded his book down onto the desk. "What's this about, sheriff?"

"You didn't happen to receive a call from Margaret this morning?"

"Can't say that I did. I was out earlier, checking

in the conditions of the trail-heads, could have just missed her."

"Crawford Miller and his wife are dead," Caudel stated with as much emotion as a stone sitting in mud.

Rundell was on his feet, brows pinched. "Dead?"

"That's right. His neighbor—Burnett—found them earlier; called us out."

"What the hell happened?"

"Something—*something* ripped them apart."

"Damn—grizzly again?"

"I …"

"Yes," Wilmont said, stepping forward, filling the silence.

The ranger looked over to Caudel who appeared locked up in his speech. "Sheriff? You okay?"

"Uh …"

"We're thinking it was a grizzly—" Wilmont continued "—possibly that one from last year."

Rundell seated himself. "Well shit. I suppose I can try my hand. I'll tell you right now though, the owners of Starlight are a tight bunch of assholes. Last time I ran into one of them when they were laying the foundation out there with a small crew, they had the gall to tell me—sheriff, you okay?"

Caudel looked on the verge of a spell. He put his hand out, steadying a swoon.

"Sheriff?" Wilmont pulled up a chair. "Rundell, get some water!"

Inexplicably dizzy, Caudel stared off at the map tacked behind Rundell's desk. There was a red circle indicating Camp Starlight.

"Sheriff—sheriff?"

Caudel looked up at the two faces staring down at him in concern. Rundell had his hands resting on his hips, his ranger badge flashing off the sun, his mustache curled up, his beady gray eyes focused.

Wilmont lowered to eye level with Caudel. "Sheriff? You alright—" he looked up to Rundell "—call the doctor, tell him—"

"I don't need a goddamn doctor," Caudel said suddenly. Forcing himself to stand, he leaned against a filing cabinet, blinking his eyes. "I don't need a doctor—I—"

Wilmont studied his face. "You certain about that?"

Rundell just stood back silent, a concern in his eyes.

Caudel swallowed. "It's not a grizzly—not a grizzly."

CHAPTER 6

"How much further up river?" Darlene asked, her red hair bloomed out over the rounded bulge of the lime-green tube beneath her, sunlight baking her pale skin pink.

Shawn nudged his black sunglasses above his eyes, his brow coming together, leaning over his tube. "Uh … I'd say we're nearly there. I see the log sticking up out of the water. Our camp should be on the other side."

"Good, I'm getting hungry."

He spread two fingers over his lips, flicking his tongue in the gap. "Me too."

Darlene laughed.

The river carried them slowly with its current. Sun sparked off the surface, birds chirped and jumped in the trees. Pines reared skyward, a few leaned crooked, the needled branches brushing the surface.

"Tonight I'm hoping to catch us some fish," Shawn said.

"Are they safe to eat?"

"Are you kidding? Fresh trout from a river is a delicacy!"

"I don't think I ever had trout."

"You'll love it—if I can catch one."

"What if you don't?"

"We can have that can of chili and … some of the deer jerky, I guess."

"We've been eating that jerky for two days," Darlene reminded him. "Please tell me we're not eating that for lunch?"

"Uh … no, I'll fix us—oh, we have some bread left over from yesterday, I'll make us a sandwich."

"What kind?"

He thought a moment. "*Tuna?*"

"Is that all we have?"

"I'm pretty sure."

Darlene sighed. "If that's all we have then."

"Sorry babe—we ate most of our food during the first night—remember?"

Darlene laughed. "Yeah, we got fucked up."

Shawn laughed. "All that beer."

Nearing the bank, Shawn reached out, grabbed hold of a branch. "I'm going to pull us ashore. Make sure your rope is secure."

Darlene tugged the rope knotted around the river-tube handle. "It's good."

Feeling the ground below his feet, his toes dug into the sediment. Rising out of his tube, he leaned over, grabbed the rope, started coiling it towards him.

"I can feel the bottom," she said. "Can you help me out?"

Shawn put a hand out to her, assisting her out

of the tube. "Damn babe, your body is *red!*"

She looked down at her self. "Damnit, I knew that sun lotion was bad!"

Shawn laughed.

"It's not funny, Shawn. You know how bad I burn!"

"I know, I'm sorry, I'm sorry" he said, stifling a laugh.

"Do you have any left?"

"What do you mean?"

"*Lotion!* Do you have any sunscreen left?" she asked impatiently.

"A little bit. But wasn't your sunscreen was supposed to be stronger than mine?"

Her eyes fell down to her arms and legs and belly, the mounds of her breasts. "I'm a fucking lobster!"

Shawn eyed her body. "If it makes you feel any better, that oily skin is sort of hot. You look fucking *hot!*"

"Ha. Ha. Thanks a lot—I feel gross."

"Come on babe," he took her by the hand. "You can sit here under the shade, you won't feel so bad."

She eased herself down on to the granule shelf that sloped into the river, above her a fan of pine limbs blotted out the sun, a wind blew over her from the river. It was cool against the skin, caused her already hard nipples to push against the white bikini top. "It does feel a little better under here— what are you staring at?"

"You!"

"Is it *that* bad?"

"Will you stop it, you look great!"

"You're just saying that."

"No, it's true. It's actually kind of … sexy."

"My pain and skin is *sexy* to you?"

"Yeah—no—uh, *you* are sexy. I'm sorry babe, but that red hair all wet like that, and your skin glowing is—yeah, it's turning me on."

Darlene laughed sheepishly. She looked up at him; her eyes traced his abs and chest, the black sunglasses and swept black hair. His shorts were soaked and dripping beads of river water into the sand around his toes. "Not looking too bad yourself."

Shawn swung his shades onto his head. "Really?"

Darlene smiled. "Come here."

Shawn looked around as though somebody were peaking at him. Looked back across the river, up into the blue sky, past Darlene into the brush at her back. His eyes traveled her body and he felt his dick bulging in his trunks. He put a thumb to his bare, wet chest. "Me?"

"Yes you idiot, who else?"

Smiling, Shawn eased his knees into the pebbly sand at her toes.

Darlene placed her hands behind her back, her fingers pulled the knot loose on her top. Her heavy breasts released. She cupped her hands below the pair, flicked the nipples. "You like 'em?"

Shawn licked his lips, thinking about the nipples in his mouth. "I *love* 'em."

"Well," she said. "What are you waiting for?"

Shawn leaned forward.

Darlene put up a hand. "Shorts first."

"Really babe? Out here?"

"You shy?" she teased.

"No—well, it just feels weird. We have a tent—"

"Hey, my tits are out, you don't see me complaining."

He rolled his shoulders. "Yeah, you're right."

Shawn wasted no time and kicked out of his trunks. His erection wilted in the wind. "Ah shit."

Darlene cupped a hand over her mouth, laughing.

"It's not funny, Dar."

She pinched her fingers together. "It's a *little* funny."

Shawn's face went red.

"Oh, I'm just messing with you," she said. "Bring it over here, I'll get it hard real fast."

Rolling his eyes, his hand blocking his limp penis, he scooted toward her.

"Stand up babe," she said. "How else am I supposed to reach it?"

Feeling flushed again, Shawn stood. "Close enough?"

She licked her lips, her fingers curled around his flaccid shaft. "Perfect." She gave him a few tugs, felt it bulk against her fingers. "Feeling happy yet?"

"Almost."

She leaned forward, spit on the head, her fingers curled over the tip, dragging the wetness down his shaft. "Better?"

He felt his cock harden. "Oh, much better."

"*Yeah?*"

"Yes."

She grabbed her nipple, pinched until she squealed, she leaned forward. "How about this?"

Shawn's eyes rolled white in his skull as her mouth sank over his cock. But it was the sounds in her throat as she swallowed down his shaft, moaning and choking on the girth that increased his excitement.

"Holy shit babe, you better slow down."

She popped it from her mouth. "Already?"

He rolled his eyes. "What do you expect?"

She smiled as she swallowed over him again. Drool bubbled around her lips as she worked harder.

"Oh shit—oh shit."

Her head drove forward, working the length faster. Strips of her wet red hair slapped against her bouncing breasts.

"Oh, I'm there, I'm there!"

Her mouth was suddenly jerked away from the shaft with a muffled yelp, leaving his dick wet and throbbing in the air.

Shawn worked his load out with a hand. "Oh babe, that felt—babe?"

Confused, Shawn looked around, his erection sagging into itself. He looked over his shoulder to the tent. "Darlene?"

What the hell, he thought.

Pulling his trunks to his waist, a sound in the bushes ahead caused him to straighten up. "Babe? That you? What are you doing in there?"

Stepping forward, his eyes on the bush, a half grin on his face. "Babe, that felt—"

A strident peal of a woman's scream sent a shiver up his body like an electric shock.

"B-babe—" The brush shook and thrashed as if a pair of strong hands were on the other side trying to yank its roots from the soil.

"Darlene!"

The agitation stopped.

Aside from the river coursing over and between polished rocks and feeding into pools; the light wind, Shawn's heart was the only other sound in that pinhole silence.

"Dar—" Something wet blew from the brush, spraying him red. Its suddenness startled him. He stood there, unmoved, solid to the earth, blood coated on him, in his mouth, in his eyes, wet in his hair. Slowly he looked down, saw the blood, then looked up into the bushy hedge of brush.

"Darlene!"

A bulk of something white and red hurled over the top of the brush, smacking him in the chest. Shawn toppled to the ground with a scream. Backing away on hands and heels, he started pealing his lungs open with a scream that frightened birds from the boughs; their black bodies clouding the sky. He continued screaming as he looked down on the mutilated torso of his girlfriend, saw one breast scooped from her chest, the other torn and hanging from a thread, a ragged bleeding hollow where her beautiful head once laughed. Red ropes and other slimy tendrils of interiors bulged from the waist, feeding into a pool of thick blood spreading in the sand.

"DARLENE!"

The bushes started again, thrashing and shaking branches.

Shawn fought the urge to sit there and brood. He raised himself, nearly going on his face as he headed for the float bobbing in the river. Throwing himself on top, he pulled at the loop of rope tethered to a broken, water logged trunk.

"Come on!" he shouted. The rope was caught in a cleft of wood that prevented him from tugging it loose. "SHIT!"

Turning out of the tube, Shawn kicked into the river, submerging to his waist and dove beneath the cool blue surface. Coming up for air, he drove his arms hard, going with the current. Fighting to the opposite side, he felt the ground, started up the slope until his body was clear and heaving with air on the bank. He wanted to call out to his girlfriend, but remembered what was left of her on the other side at their camp.

Looking out across the billowy ribbon of river, he saw the blood feeding into the water, the torso, but then saw something black and big between a group of trees. He shielded his brow. "What—what the fuck—" It moved out of sight, melting back into the woods. "Fuck!"

Immediately, he was thinking it was a bear, and felt relatively safe at the moment across the river as he thought of a way to free himself. Left without shoes or gear, he was in a world of difficulty. With six miles of heavy forest between him and his car, the pain in his chest only increased. He felt his eyes water as he looked on the torso again.

Darlene…

Something moved behind him in a clump of sun baked boulders; dense pines and brush rising around it.

Swallowing, his mouth open, he felt his body quiver and shake, anticipating some monster bear emerging from the woods, looming upright on the boulders, strips of flesh dripping from the tips of its red teeth, blood in its fur.

Slowly, he backed away, back to the river, his eyes roaming the woods to his front, the sun burning his back, water lapping at his ankles. A snap to his right swung his eyes wide. Another to his left, like a thrown stone smacking a trunk, caused him to shout out in frustration. Then the woods came alive as if ready to upend and crash down on top of him; something else roared over the shaking of the woods, the ground beneath him seemed to agitate and shift.

Then silence.

Crouched in the water, his hands pressed

against his head, he looked around warily. Lowering his hands to his side, he raised himself out of the crouch. "I'm going insane."

A crash of timber splintered, brush blew apart as a colossal, black hairy thing on two legs like pine trunks came dashing out of the woods, arms spread open wide from a barrel shaped torso, claws hooked, eyes alive with red fire. An earth cracking scream roared from its spiked mouth as it stampeded forward, crunching limbs and breaking stones.

Shawn fell back into the water, shrieking when a hairy claw clamped to his ankle. He fought and kicked and screamed at the beast, but was dragged quickly out of the water; felt the gravity go out from under him as he left the ground. His world oscillated and spun as he was lifted and swung forward onto a boulder where his head popped apart like a rotten melon. Blood and brain shot into the woods, splashed a grisly pattern on the boulder. Another swing of the limp body in its massive arm, the beast hammered Shawn against the broad stone like a blacksmith striking an anvil, over and over until his bones poked from his flesh and blood poured out of a hundred wounds.

Emptied of most things that keep a man living, the beast flung the flaccid sack of bones into the woods with an ear shattering roar.

CHAPTER 7

Wilmont took the wheel after Caudel had his spell in the ranger station. He was concerned that maybe something medical had occurred with the sheriff, and that fact alone was pertinent enough to hurry along this business and get him to the doctor back in town.

Caudel stared out the window, watching pines flash by, knowing in his head he was well and coherent, not ravaged by illness as he knew his deputy suspected him to be.

Silence was in the rig. Sun flushed the interior with its heat, dust billowed behind, obscuring Rundell's truck in the rearview which was trailing them to the camp.

"I think it's for your own good, sheriff. I care about you, okay? Back in the station—"

"I'm fine deputy."

Wilmont had his doubts. "You say you're fine, but back at the Miller's—"

"What about the Miller's?"

"Well, you looked sort of—sorta' out of it if I'm honest about it."

"Just tired deputy, ain't nothing more to it.

You're bringing shit into this that ain't there."

Wilmont nodded. "Back at the station sheriff—"

"Look, Wilmont—I'm tired. I didn't sleep so well last night after the quake shook my house. And that goddamn sun ain't helping things any, and the bodies …"

"Probably be a good thing to see the doc, sheriff, just to be safe an all."

"Ain't nothing wrong with me son, how many goddamn times do I have to tell you that? Do I look like some invalid to you?"

Wilmont looked over at him, saw the fire back in those gray eyes.

"Do I!"

"No, I suppose you don't, sheriff, I—"

"Look, I get enough shit from my own kids when they call and check on me every goddamn night to make sure I'm still breathing. I don't need another fucking nurse checking my pulse every goddamn minute of the day."

One thing about the sheriff, Wilmont knew, was that he would never compare him with another man of his age. Caudel was a head-strong man, with the power of young muscles in his body and a constitution that would rival most. After a life conditioned in the woods, age seemed trivial, as long as one put in the work required of hard living in those woods. So maybe Wilmont was looking for an issue where there was none to be found. Instead of breathing down the sheriff's neck, maybe it would be beneficial if he allowed

Caudel his space—maybe then if there were any more strange occurrences, then he'd force his perspective on him, until then, he decided to drop any impending concerns.

"Understood, sheriff."

The gate to the camp was a flimsy affair; a single column of wood lay across that required an arm to lift and move aside. There were no fencing or security measures put in place that Wilmont or Caudel could detect. They drove on in beneath a weaving of boughs, shaded from the sun. Fifty feet in, they spotted the camp, which, on first appearance, was a pathetic crowd of inferior construction and negligence.

"This is the great camp starlight?" Wilmont asked perplexed at the layout. "What did they do with all that money they supposedly sank into this place?"

Caudel kept silent and let his eyes wander.

There was a small bus parked in front of a building which Wilmont figured was the central part of the camp, something like an assembly hall or rather a cafeteria lodge, maybe both. He eased the rig behind the bus, shutting off the engine. Rundell's brakes screeched as he pulled in behind them.

"Not seeing anybody," Wilmont remarked.

"Probably indoors."

After the three dismounted and gathered

together, they stood around, faces roaming the land.

"Ain't no point standing around like a bunch of assholes, I say we spread out, find somebody we can talk to."

"Sounds good to me, sheriff," Rundell agreed, fixing the badge on his chest.

"I'll take that main building there," Wilmont pointed out.

"I'll check by the lake," Rundell said.

"I'll head for the cabins," Caudel told them. "When we do find life here, we bring them back to this point—to the bus—where we can discuss things, copy?"

The two nodded.

"One other thing before we go: we remain calm. As much as I wish I could march in here and wrap a chain around the place and be done with this mess, this is a delicate situation. It requires brains, not muscle. We approach these people in an easy manner, get them on our side. Any questions?"

"None sheriff."

"Okay, lets spread out."

While both Rundell and Wilmont went about their search of the lake and main hall building, Caudel walked beneath the shade of pines still unrevealed by the sun's scorching reach.

Damn, he thought, *if only I had the sense—the voice—to say what it is I need to say, and say it in a way to convince those men to take me serious, and not think me some goddamn loon, which is precisely what'd they call me.*

Even if they hadn't come outright with such a cruel word, the looks alone would suggest the term, being eyes can sometimes be more cruel then vocals. Caudel figured it would give them a reason to further press him for medical help, which his deputy had been hinting about for some time now.

If that sonofabitch only knew what I saw; knew what it did to those Indians back so long ago, then maybe he'd think twice before branding me and considering a straight jacket.

God how he wanted to tell him, and maybe he should; hell, he almost blabbed like a drunk to them stupid kids who he was sure were already miles into the woods looking for a nice level spot to pop a tent under the stars and drown themselves in booze around a raging fire.

"Dumb ass kids," he said to himself.

"Can I help you?"

Caudel turned to the voice; a pleasant voice that sounded much like his own daughter. A woman filled his eyes. She was a young thing, younger than his daughter, maybe early twenties, golden ribbons of blond hair down her shoulders, big blue eyes full of life, a slim athletic figure. She was wearing a green shirt, a pair of short white shorts that showed well the muscles of her bronzed legs, a pair of timber boots with red laces.

Caudel removed his stetson, placed it over his chest. "Afternoon ma'am, my name is sheriff Roy Caudel, from Starbright Springs, I'm looking for the owner, or director—somebody in charge around here."

The woman looked confused for a moment. "Um ... well, it's just me and five other counselors at the moment—oh, and Dean, our bus driver, but he's getting ready to leave. I'm not sure when Pete —the owner—will be showing up."

"And what's your name?"

Brittney smiled. "Oh, sorry, I'm Brittney— Brittney Gatten."

"That's a pretty name, Brittney. Is there any way I can be put in touch with this Pete character?"

Brittney shook her head. "There's no working phones up here at the moment, not really sure why, we were told there would be communications up here; even our radio is acting up. It's picking up channels, sort of, but not so well."

Caudel nodded. "I understand. It's the trees, the mountains, all of it interfering."

"I guess."

"When do you expect the kids to arrive?" he asked.

"We were just thinking that ourselves a moment ago. Dean said his partner was bringing them up before nightfall, so we're expecting them any moment."

Shit. "Do you happen to know what time they may have—"

"*Sheriff!*"

Caudel turned, saw Rundell waving at him, three men standing beside him.

"Those the other counselors," he asked Brittney.

She looked past the sheriff. "Yes sir, that's them. I have two other's with me—they're up in the cabin getting changed."

"Mind getting them for me? I'll wait right here for you three."

"Not at all."

"Much obliged."

"Says his name is sheriff … Oh, I forgot—Caudel, that was it!"

"What's he want?" Angela asked, pulling a yellow shirt over her bare chest.

"I don't know, he seems nice; a little anxious too."

Julie was marking something in her book with a thick highlighter. "Give me one second."

Brittney pushed aside the green wool drapes, saw the man standing out there facing the lake. He was a kind looking older man. Short gray hair, a scruff of gray points on his chin and around his lips. His skin was weathered bronze. He looked powerful for his age, healthy too.

"Okay," Julie said. "Ready."

The three walked down the pine needle carpeted walk.

"Sheriff?"

Caudel swung away from the lake.

"We're ready."

After introductions, the four of them walked over to join the others. During the brief stroll, Angela spoke up.

"What's this about, sheriff?"

"It's Angela right?" he asked.

"Right."

"Well, Angela, seems we're having trouble with some wildlife (*life that ain't from these goddamn woods*) and earlier today it hurt some people—real bad. (*Butchered them something awful*)."

"Oh that's terrible," she said. "I hope they're doing well."

The other girls gasped.

"We were thinking—kinda' hoping—to maybe bring this camp to an early close; that is until we can locate and contain this animal (*which may never happen, considering it's a foul and unspeakable thing*)."

"It's that bad?" Julie asked, somewhat frightened by the notion.

"Yes ma'am, I'm afraid so."

Brittney saw two men, one clothed like the sheriff, around her father's age, dark hair, dark brows, animated with the counselors. The other man was tall and was wearing an all green uniform. He had a gray mustache and dark hair.

"That your partner?" she asked.

"It is. The short one there, that's my deputy, Deputy Clint Wilmont. The other man—one with the mustache—is a local ranger, name of Jim Rundell."

As they got closer, Caudel could hear Wilmont's voice rising hot against a big sack of muscle with black hair who had his bulging arms folded over his chest.

"I'm telling you for the last time meat-head, we're worried about a grizzly in this area that already killed a local couple, now how about you put a plug in that nasty language of yours and put me in contact with the owner of this place!"

Goddamnit, Caudel thought. *Here I am trying to be light with the situation; ambassadorial and all— to get these people to cooperate without issues—and Wilmont's shouting at these men as if he were aiming to read 'em their rights!*

"What the hell is goin' on deputy?"

Wilmont's face was seamed, Caudel had never seen him so mad. "Just a bit of attitude, sheriff, from this one here" he said without taking his eyes off the wall of muscle.

"Simmer down deputy—you, what's your name?"

"Marcus—"

"Well, Marcus, cat's out the bag, what my deputy here says is truth, there's a real dangerous animal around here—"

"Look, I understand that sir—" Marcus said a bit too haughty for Caudel's taste "—but I don't know what you want us to do. None of us have any authority to lock this place down. I can't even reach the owner!"

"Pete?" Caudel asked.

"That's right."

"You have a phone number where I can reach him?"

Marcus thought it over. "Yeah—yeah, in the dining hall over there, in his office. But the phones aren't working—"

"I just need the number, son. Mind going and getting it for me?"

Marcus thought about saying something in return that would get him in trouble, but after looking into those old, hard eyes, he figured it was probably better to keep any comments about the law to himself.

"Yeah, I'll go get it. Be right back."

Caudel pulled his deputy aside from the others, addressed him in a low voice.

"What the fuck was that?"

"What?"

"You trying to get these folks riled up so they won't help us out?"

"You said you wanted this place closed down, that's what I'm trying to do!"

"Pissing off these young men and women ain't how it's going to happen. As much as I wish I can manhandle this myself, we have to use our goddamn heads. We have kids inbound to this place, likely already almost here."

"I apologize sheriff, but that stack of meat over there started giving me and Rundell lip the moment he saw our badges."

Caudel figured it was more than just a spit of lip that got his blood boiling like it had. Figured it was a combination of the young man's attitude and maybe his own evasion of Wilmont's questioning and suspicions that added to his sudden outburst.

"Well, let's get back to Rundell before he bores them to death."

Rundell was speaking softly with the counselors, assuring them that all would be okay just so long as they took precautions and remained vigilant.

"Was it really a bear?" asked Brittney wide eyed.

Caudel looked to his partner, to Rundell, then to Brittney. "It's a dangerous *animal*, that much we're aware about. I'm sorry to say that it did kill a local couple earlier today, and we're concerned about the camp being opened while this beast is on the loose you understand—"

"But bears don't actively attack humans," a red headed counselor told Caudel.

"What's your name?" Caudel questioned him.

"Ron."

"Well, *Ron*, when a bear gets a taste of human blood, it can turn them feral and dangerous as all hell, and right now that animal is out in those woods, blood in its belly, doing god knows what right now. That's why we deem the closure of this camp critical."

"Have it right here," Marcus said, running up, waving a sheet of paper in his fist.

Caudel grabbed it from him. "Thank you." He looked it over, then put his eyes on the crowd of counselors silent before him. "We're going to head over to the ranger station down the road, ring this number up. Once we get a hold of this Pete fella, we'll be in contact; either way, we'll be in contact. Shouldn't be long."

Brittney stepped forward. "What do we do in the meantime sheriff?"

Caudel folded the paper, stuffed it into his pocket. "In the meantime ... I suggest you all pack your bags, get in that bus, and head back where you came from. I'll wait outside this gate if I have to and turn those kids around myself."

With that, Caudel put his back to the counselors and jumped behind the wheel of the rig. "Come on deputy."

"Coming sheriff."

Rundell walked by, jumped into his own rig.

Both motors roared alive. Both wound out of the courtyard and headed for the narrow path leading back to the main forest service road.

Suddenly, a big yellow box filled the road ahead of Caudel, sunlight winking off its windshield. He nudged his truck aside as the bus barreled past him, the faces of kids pressed against the glass, followed by a similar bus but painted white and packed with what Caudel assumed were staffing for the camp.

Rundell hit his horn after the bus passed them both, left his truck running, footed it over to

Caudel's rig.

"You see him?" he asked, hyper in his voice.

"The kids?"

"No, the other guy—the driver? It was Pete."

"Well," Caudel said looking over to his partner. "Let's not loose our cool."

CHAPTER 8

He was a heavyset man, not one conditioned for the rocky and uneven terrain that swept around him. Sweat clung to the folds of his body, something he kept dabbing with a sodden kerchief. Dressed in a pair of beige shorts that threatened to split as he crouched on the edge of a precipice, Horace made use of the thick brush that crowned the ledge, belting him in to its greenery.

It was the perfect spot, one that shielded him from the sun that sought out his exposed skin and lashed it with its burning kiss. Above and behind him were tightly packed pine columns that waved slightly at the wind whipping along the boughs and branches, shaking the occasional pine cone loose to tap and roll lightly over a bed of desiccating pine needles.

The soil beneath his feet was soft and cool, which aided his knees as they were burrowing into its crust. His blue shirt was soaked black with sweat, and around his neck was a thick leather band which tethered to the Nikon 35mm with extended lens which currently filled his hands.

"Oh baby, just like that," he said. "Come on now,

show Horace what your mother gave you—that's it now, come out—come on." He focused the iris, snapped a shot just as the woman below, in the calm cove of a river artery burst from the placid surface in a shower of crystal beads. "Oh, perfect, perfect. You were blessed, oh were you blessed."

The woman swept her wet brown hair out of her eyes, pushed the globes of her sun sparked breasts together and encouraged a black haired man across from her to leave the shade of the bank and join her in the cool water.

Horace couldn't hear much about what they were saying, but he figured that was pretty much the gist of what the conversation entailed, considering the man now helped himself out of his shorts and dove beneath the surface, swimming over to the girl who suddenly screamed as he came up out of the water with her naked body in his arms, crushing kisses to her face.

The couple on the crescent beach facing their friends were laughing, listening to a song Horace couldn't make out from his spot on the ledge. He zeroed his lens on the blond with a blue bikini two piece animated with the guy beside her who had a dome of big brown hair and was wearing a pair of ragged cut off jeans and opened red plaid shirt, shoe-less, leaning back on his elbows.

Focusing his lens on the woman, his eyes traced her thick blond hair which was pinched into twin tails which were currently tossed behind her, allowing the exposure of her large breasts to be cooked by the sun. One of her legs was bent at the knee, slightly wedged to the side which Horace focused on intently and snapped a shot of the cleft of her sex which was prominent and lighted by the sun.

"Oh I bet its wet, wetter than that water there. I bet its warm too, nice and hot." Another snap of the camera and he cursed in a low voice. "Damnit, out of film." Reaching the pouch on his hip for an extra roll, a sound in the bush behind him gave his fingers pause. His eyes wandered. "Damn squirrels."

Sweating with the exertion of keeping himself silent and his presence a secret, his fat fingers wrapped the small blunt roll of a film canister. "Gotcha'" he said, somewhat relieved. Opening the rear of the camera, his knee slipped from the groove, causing him to start forward. Fumbling with the camera, his hands instinctively sought the dirt, keeping his body upright, regrettably freeing the camera which tumbled from his hands and flipped and flopped down the slanting shelf ledge where it plunged into the placid clear blue water below.

"*Shit!*" he stammered "*Shit, shit— shitshitshitshit!*"

Melissa, grappling with Frank, her breasts seeming to float on the surface, looked behind her at the sudden splash. "What was that?" she asked.

Frank took advantage of her curiosity and grabbed her breast, filling his hand with the soft slick mound, the nipple poking between his fingers.

"Ouch—not now!" she said.

"Oh come on baby, I'm sure it was just a fish, maybe a pine cone from the trees up there."

"No, it sounded too heavy."

"Probably a rock then, come on baby."

Her eyes walked up the sheer wall of rock and shrubs, roving the ledge and brush that trimmed its top; to the pine trees that waved lightly in the wind.

"Yeah, whatever," she said, turning back to Frank.

"*Fuck!*" Horace whispered loudly. "Fucking camera cost me two thousand dollars!"

Staring angrily at the naked woman in the water, to the bikini covered blond on the beach; he felt his penis bulk, thought of the knife on his hip. "If only those damn guys weren't around, then we'd have some real fun."

Overcome with a thought, his face dropped as he looked around behind him then slowly worked his zipper down, fumbling in the dark interior of his shorts for the nugget of his hardening penis.

Finding the mushroom-like bulge, he started to free it, but then something shifted behind him. He turned, would have screamed—maybe he had—if his face hadn't been swallowed over by a gaping black mouth crammed with spikes that crunched its way through his skull freeing his rotund body to fall forward and smack the earth with a meaty sound which aided to disgorge a river of blood from the red hollow of his neck where its scarlet trail rushed down the slope, parting past brush and around stones and roots to trickle and pebble the surface of the cove waters below.

Charlotte sat forward, her knees coming together, reaching out a hand to silence the radio. She looked around, up towards the cliff above the cove. "Did you hear something?"

"I hear Melissa and Frank down in the water splashing and shouting."

"No, I thought I heard—thought I heard a scream in the woods up there," she pointed to the cliff.

Greg dropped his head forward, away from the sky, put his shades up on his head. "I don't see anything."

"I didn't *see* anything," she told him, "I said I *heard* something."

Greg swung the shades down, leaned back into the sun again. "You probably just heard Melissa—or Greg."

Charlotte kept her eyes on the cliff, looking for any unnatural angle or suspicious movement. "I think we should look for a spot to camp soon."

"We have plenty of time to look for a camp site, might as well enjoy this sun while we can."

"Yeah, but I would like to *not* be looking for firewood in the dark or setting up the tent in the dark, so I think its a good idea if we get going soon."

"Come on Charlotte, another ten minutes."

"Okay," she relented after a pause, "but in ten minutes you better not ask for another twenty minutes."

"I promise, ten minutes and we'll pack this up and get moving. Besides, I know of a place, not too far from here according to the map. Looks nice and open and sits on a small lake."

"That sounds nice."

"Should be."

Charlotte stared off at Melissa and Frank in the river pool, thrashing and playing with each other. "You really think the sheriff was joking? That there really isn't a bear out there?"

Greg sighed. "Again with the bear business? He never said it was a bear."

Charlotte rolled her eyes in thought. "I guess I'm just assuming that's what he meant by dangerous animal, I'm pretty sure he's not talking about a squirrel or a raccoon."

"Could be a mountain lion," Greg suggested. "A cougar or something like that."

"Oh I really don't want to hear that."

"Calm down Charlotte. I dunno' what the hell that sheriff was talking about, but so what if its a bear or a mountain lion or whatever; what are the chances of us running into a dangerous animal out here in the woods? If you haven't noticed, the area is *huge*. I'm pretty sure animals like that don't like big crowds and lots of noise."

Charlotte's shoulders sank. "I guess you're right, but—"

"Look, Frank has his gun, we'll be fine. Nothing around these woods is going to stand there after he fires that thing off; they'll go off scampering away, trust me."

Charlotte nodded. "Okay, but I'm still worried, just a little."

"Don't be—ain't nothing out there, besides, we dispose of our food the right way, there won't be anything for that bear, or whatever it is, to track us."

"Yeah, I suppose."

"Now, enough of that sheriff and the animal, hand me a beer."

Five black claws sank into the pudgy meat of the back. With ease, it peeled away the spine in a meaty gash that opened the man's back in a swell of blood. Flies started around the air, a halo of black ringing the beast as its teeth filed along the reddened, gristly column of vertebrae.

Casting aside the limp spine, it plunged its hairy black hands into the cavity, separating the man in a yawning of red tethers; meat and blood filled the gap in a wave. It brought a slab of the fat man's body horizontally to its blood splashed grin. Its teeth clamped and jerked loose flanks, masticating the meat, clumps of yellow fat stuck in its hairy face. It's eyes burned red as the blood and meat engorged its belly.

Continuing its feast, it knew that even the bounty of flesh heaped below it, would not long sustain its hunger.

CHAPTER 9

Sheriff Caudel hammered his fist down onto the surface of his desk hard enough to cause all the contents on top of it to rise in the air an inch and come back down scattered.

"That no good sonofabitch," he shouted. "Tried and threaten me—you—and Rundell with a goddamn lawsuit if we were to set foot on his camp again. I'm the goddamn law around here, what gives that fat bellied city boy the authority to speak to me in such a discourteous manner!"

Deputy Wilmont sat on the edge of his desk, arms folded across his chest. "I had a feeling that lousy prick would try his hand at a lawsuit; he sure fits the type, and his buddy boy counselor I'm thinking needs a good set of knuckles to the chin."

Caudel wore a hole in the ground behind his desk, pacing back and forth, scratching at his chin, eyes inflamed with anger.

"It's all about money goddamnit, that sonofabitch is worried about his bank account after we go and tell him some animal is out on the loose, blood hungry and dangerous. We warn him that the kids were in danger, and he just stands there with that fat smiling face of his, telling us we're overreacting!"

Wilmont thought maybe the sheriff was overreacting a pinch. After all, during the investigation of the hikers up at Bald Ridge last year, he couldn't remember the sheriff acting out of character, raging and snapping like he was now, ordering closures and stuttering and having spells. On the contrary, Caudel was collected and calm and ordered.

Earlier at the camp, he had reverted to that cool and collected personality whom Wilmont instantly recognized and respected. It was that same collected order he knew the sheriff for, but then the argument with the camp owner Pete, he again came unglued and unstable and lashed out with words that frightened even Wilmont. Though not a saint himself in any regards, getting worked up over that counselor probably wasn't his best decision at the time.

Even though that slimeball was asking for it.

He was seriously having doubts about the composition of Caudel's mental state. But he promised himself to reel back; to stay away from injecting personal feelings into the matter, but the sheriff was making it difficult on him. Could he allow a man he believed to be on the decline remain in control? Or perhaps it was Wilmont that underestimated the urgency of the situation.

"You have any suggestions sheriff?"

Caudel stared out the window of his office; out

at the slowly sinking sun in the west. "Yeah, one."

Caudel left his office behind, stormed down the short corridor. Emerging out of the hall, he put his eyes on the dispatch station. "Margaret, ring that old fart Thomas and tell him to hurry over to the station; he's got night watch tonight."

Margaret looked on the sheriff, stunned by the order.

"Oh, and if that ol' piss bag gives you any lip, you just tell him I know about that *still* on his property."

Margaret nodded. "Right away sheriff."

Caudel turned, saw Wilmont a foot away, a look of confusion on his face.

"What the hell you doing, sheriff?"

"Grab a rifle out of that rack there and grab me a shotgun and fill your pockets with ammo."

"What sort of plan you have hatching in that head of yours?"

Caudel put those burning coals of his on the deputy. "That Pete character don't want us to step inside his property, fine by me. But he has no jurisdiction *outside* that camp. That's my land, and I aim to keep it safe."

CHAPTER 10

Brittney never would have imagined that sheriff coming unglued like he had. He had an easy speaking manner when he was addressing her and her peers earlier in the day, but after Pete rolled up with the kids and cooking staff, put a finger in his face and started all sorts of legal threats, diplomacy was out the window after the sheriff grew red faced and let loose a string of four lettered variants that made her flush and stiffen up. His voice was loud and echoed over the camp; even his deputy and that forest ranger guy shrank back a step; the kids were smiling, some were even laughing about the exchange, but others looked genuinely frightened.

"You okay over there Brittney?"

Brittney looked up from the tray of food below her, saw Angela staring over at her. She had a bulge of food in her cheek. "Yeah, just thinking about earlier."

"With the sheriff?"

Brittney nodded. "Kind of crazy, huh?"

"Yeah, that was pretty hectic," she laughed

nervously.

"I thought it was pretty unprofessional of him honestly," Julie stated, forking some peas into her mouth.

"He was just concerned about the kids—I don't think Pete or Marcus did anything to help the issue."

"You ask me, I think that old man needs to go home and take a nap. He shouldn't have been screaming the way he was—especially in front of the children like that."

"I don't think Pete should have been pointing a finger in his face and acting like he was either; threatening action if he were to step on 'private property' again. I mean, the man's a sheriff, he has to have some say in the manner, right?"

Julie and Angela remained silent.

"You girls talking about that sheriff again?" It was Jake, his blond hair was still damp from when he took the kids down to the lake earlier for swimming. He placed his tray beside her own, swung back a chair and settled himself down.

"Just talking about what happened."

"I think Pete did the right thing," he told her. "I don't think that sheriff was right in the head. Those small town types always seem to have a chip on their shoulder about something; and when 'outsiders' come stomping around, they generally raise all sorts of shit over it. I've seen it before—not in any of the summer camps, but during hikes and camping trips with friends."

Brittney had camped all over the state with her parents and she couldn't ever remember a time when they were harassed by local lawmen or anybody populating small towns. In fact, they had ran into many nice and caring individuals that assisted them with any of the myriad questions her father put to them.

"I can't say I ever ran into people like that."

"Yeah, well, now you have."

Marcus was walking up, Ron on his tail. Both were smiling and pointing at campers ringed about tables cramming jaws with hamburgers and fries and brownies and chips. The dining hall was a raucous of voices and laughter; tables crowded with young faces. Last count put the camper roster at thirty-five, but from the sound rising and falling inside the dining hall, you would think there were double if not triple that number massed inside.

Marcus walked up, placed his tray beside Jake, straddled over a chair and set his weight into it and smiled. "What's going on people?"

Jake drank deeply off a Pepsi bottle. "Nothing much, we were just talking about that sheriff—"

"Oh man, that guy was getting on my last nerves, what an asshole. What the hell was his problem anyways?"

"He's worried about the kids," Brittney said. "Isn't it obvious?"

Marcus laughed. "Has a funny way of showing it. Cussing and screaming in front of the kids; he was acting like a child himself—*worse* than a child."

"You weren't giving him much of a choice," Brittney pointed out.

Marcus put his eyes on her. "What do you mean?"

"I mean that you and Pete were pretty condescending; threatening him with a lawsuit; it looked like you two were enjoying it, purposely antagonizing him for the concerns he had."

Marcus put his hands up. "I was just backing Pete up; he *is* the owner here; it *is* his property. You can't allow those backwoods type police hillbillies to get in your face like he was; they have the support of the town, if they pushed it, they could have this place closed down permanently—not anytime soon, but it could happen in the future."

"I don't think the way you two were acting was helping the situation any; and you say he shouldn't have acted like that in front of the children, but the two of *you* were acting like it was past your *own* nap time."

"Damn, Brittney, you have an eye for this guy or something?" Marcus laughed. "He was being a jerk —"

Brittney leaned forward. "Maybe if you two were *listening* to him instead of threatening him, you would have thought what he had to say was pretty reasonable. Remember the dangerous animal that's still out there after *killing* that couple, or did you forget!"

A silence arrested the room.

Brittney felt a sea of faces turned to her. She hadn't realized how loud her voice had gotten, echoing in the rafters.

She swallowed, adjusted her seat.

Jake turned to face the campers. "Hey, why did it get so quiet in here? Come on kids, finish those meals so we can all get ready for the campfire tonight. Who likes ghost stories?"

A few hands shot up.

"Good, good, because as you can see, Brittney here was just telling us a great one she can't wait to scare you all with. Am I right Brittney?"

Brittney felt the red in her face. "Uh … *right.*"

As sudden as that silence settled over the room, it was quickly dispelled by a rising of murmuring and laughing amongst the children again; the sound of utensils scraping trays.

Marcus lowered his head over his tray, his voice soft. "Not wise to scream about things in front of the kids, wouldn't you say Brittney?"

Brittney shoved her chair back, stood, grabbed her tray, and marched off, doing her best to keep a smile on her face as she weaved around the tables cluttered with campers.

Laying her tray on a stack of empties, a hand cupped her shoulder. She turned, saw Ron, a smile on his face. "Are you okay?"

"Yeah, I'm good—just—"

"What?"

"I'm just worried."

"About the animal?"

"Yeah, aren't you? Is *anybody?*"

"I wouldn't worry about it, Brittney, really. I've studied the animals of this area and none of them are that dangerous, I mean, unless you threaten their offspring or invade their feeding areas, but … we're in a campground—"

"With no fencing I might add."

"Yes, but that doesn't mean you should worry about it. I don't know if I agree with Pete and Marcus on this one but honestly, I would let it go."

"Am I supposed to let it go if a child or one of us is hurt by this animal?"

"No, that's not what I meant. What I'm trying to say is that animals rarely attack people, and if there was an animal attack, whose to say that the people it injured—"

"*Killed*, Ron."

"Okay, killed; whose to say they didn't do something to aggravate it? What I'm saying is, it could just be a freak case, so I wouldn't worry about some bloodthirsty grizzly or whatever to come stampeding through here and hurting people."

Brittney looked out across the mass of children. For as far back as she could remember, she had been easily seduced into panic by rumors; easily scared. Alarms were ringing in her head, but after what Ron said, the panic seemed unjustified. Maybe she *was* being paranoid for no reason. Maybe Ron was correct about this one. During all the years she camped with her folks, there had never been an instance where they feared the animals of nature; it was the two legged varieties that were the real danger in the world.

But, something about the way the sheriff carried himself earlier and during the argument, the empathy behind his words, all of it sounded legitimate, not the voice of a lunatic or the wayward or the voice of the locals.

Considering Pete had left shortly after the conflict with the sheriff, there wasn't a whole lot she could do about it, not that she'd be able to have much sway proffering her own worries to the man. So, instead she set her jaw, left the noise of the dining hall behind her, and proceeded to the cabin to prepare for the coming campfire.

CHAPTER 11

Charlotte poked at the fire with the blackened end of a twig. She pushed at the coals glowing white in the center beneath a nest of straggling flames.

"I think we're going to need more firewood—and soon."

Greg pulled deeply, crushing his can and tossing the empty into the flames. "Is that your subtle way of telling me I need to get off my ass and go find some more?"

Charlotte smiled, firelight putting an orange glow to her face. "Maybe."

"Ask Frank—Frank!"

"Quiet down," she scolded him. "You know what they're doing out there."

Greg smiled. "Oh yeah—lucky bastard."

"What's that supposed to mean?"

"I mean, well—I've heard stories."

"About Melissa?"

Greg nodded, peeled open another beer, took a pull, foam on his lips. "That's right."

Charlotte nudged at the flames, tossed in a handful of brittle twigs that quickly caught. "Like what?"

"Oh come on, Charlotte, don't act like you don't know about her."

Charlotte shuffled the twigs into the coals. "I guess I've heard things, but I don't believe they're true."

"They are," Greg stated, grinning. "According to Frank anyhow."

"And you get off on these little tales, right?"

"I didn't say I got off on it—"

"Your face says enough."

"Oh come on, Char, I didn't mean it that way—"

"Well, then what the hell did you mean?"

Greg stared into the fire. "I meant, it would be nice if maybe you did those things."

"Like what?" she asked, narrowing her eyes.

Greg smiled, pictured things in his head. "It's nothing."

"That's not fair!"

"What isn't?"

"I can see you thinking about things, Greg," she told him. "Is it because I don't do that ... one *particular* thing?"

One time she had. Her head weaved and bobbed as though she were plucking apples from a barrel, but since that time, she was done with that contest.

"That's not it, Char—"

"Really?"

"I dunno'... maybe."

Silence gapped them. Greg looked above, to

the moon, saw it hanging above those crouching black crags beyond the lake. A wind pushed off the surface, blowing at the flames, agitating ash. Around them, the woods held the shadows pursued by the firelight.

"I'll go get some wood," Greg said, rising and leaving Charlotte to brood.

"Right here?"

"You see a better place?"

Her eyes labored to open the dark that enfolded over the both of them. "I guess it's okay."

Frank smoothed out a blanket. "Babe, mind putting that flashlight over here so I can see what the hell I'm doing."

Melissa pointed the beam at him.

"Not at me—right here," he pointed.

Lowering the light, she watched him. "Are you sure it's okay to be this far from them?"

"Yeah, why not?"

"Well—"

"You're not afraid are you?"

Melissa put the light in his face. "I'm not afraid!"

Frank laughed. "Is that right?"

"Well—maybe a little."

Finished, Frank drew his shirt over his head, tossed it to the ground, took her in his arms. "I told you, baby, I'll protect you."

She kissed him. "You will?"

His fingers traced up her back. "Of course—" he

stood back, puffed his chest out, flexed his arms "—look at these guns, you really think something is going to come along and challenge these babies?"

She laughed. "You're such a fool."

He pulled her close, crushing her body to his. "Yeah, well, that's why you love me."

Not a moment passed when she found herself flat on her back, moonlight on her bare skin, legs wedged wide and Frank buried deep inside. Grunting, he worked himself, dredging and excavating her plush warm walls. Her nails bit into his back; her breathing gone heavy over his shoulder.

A sound, like a snapped twig, discouraged her fun. "What was that?"

Frank, oblivious to the sound from the woods, continued hammering his solid shaft into her hole.

She drove a fist into his gut.

"Ow, what the fuck, babe?"

"Listen …"

"What the hell am I listening for?" he asked, cheated of his fun.

"I … I heard something—" she grabbed the light, put its beam in the woods "—over there, I heard something move."

"Babe, it's probably a squirrel or a raccoon or something."

The column of light cut the dark, revealing green where there was shadow. The woods loomed and leaned over them, a wall of black with many mysteries.

"I'm not seeing anything babe; you're hearing things."

She stared over the beam, following its path. "I … I dunno, I thought I heard footsteps or something."

"Well I'm not hearing anything babe," Frank plugged his meat back into her, and the light fell from her fingers with a gasp.

"Oh, you like that?"

Her eyes rolled, "It was surprising."

Coated in sweat, the exertion continued beneath the moonlight.

From in the woods it stared, leering and hungry —a ravenous appetite salivating its tongue. In cautious strides, it flitted amongst the columned pines as a shadowed gale, or the spectral whisper of speculations. Cautious in its approach, the beast avoided brush and bramble, picking a route unmolested by needles and cones. For all its bulk, it hurtled in silence, until a foot upon the fornicating couple, its inhuman bellow shattered their lust.

"JESUSFUCKINGCHRIST!" Frank screamed the moment he watched that solid and hulking black monster curl those thick hairy fingers around the width of his girlfriend—fingers that cuffed her body like a can. Lifting her from the ground as though she were weightless, the beast thundered a roar that turned her brown hair white and her eyes into incomprehensible wells of fear. She screamed as she neared the mouth that sprung open in a chasm of moonlit fangs.

Backing away from that abominable beast, Frank scrambled amongst his clothing and gear, searching in desperation for the pistol he knew lay close. But in the turgid shadows and the terror weakening his heart, he groped blindly, cursing and stammering.

Melissa cried out in agony as the points of its claws sank beneath her flesh, crushing her bones, opening rifts along her skin. Blood burst from seams and clotted the hair of the beast in a fine mist. Its fist tightened until the knobs of red bones spoked between its fingers, and blood ran sinuously from her eyes.

Finding his pistol, Frank worked off the safety, brought up the muzzle and captured in his eye was a horror that momentarily restrained his hand. Melissa, upended like a can of beer, was fed into that masticating maw like a log in a wood chipper. Blood curtained down its chest and spattered between its knees. Its throat bulged in hideous knots. Down to her waist, her legs kicked and jerked as though she still held onto life.

In a brief instant, Frank recovered his mind, and thrust his pistol into that hairy, blooded breast. A flash drew away the night as the pistol clapped in his fist, yet the beast remained, unimpeded to the lead buried and burning inside its flesh. Another echoing report of the pistol jumped the slide expelling an empty smoking shell, and again, the thing fed and chewed and mutilated the meat and bones clogging the bowl of its mouth.

Frank fell to his knees at the sight of the monster, and the rapid absence of his girlfriend. Naked, the wind whipped him, and his eyes traveled up the broad black body. Blood and smudges of flesh in its hair and chips of bone stained its breast and face, and its mighty head lowered, and its eyes, burning with radiant crimson fire, bore him with its baleful glare.

Screaming, he raised the pistol; rounds smacked the flesh until the slide locked back empty, brass casings smoking at his toes. Caught in the frailty of insanity, Frank cackled drunkenly, before rising and running with madness in his throat, back to the camp—back to his friends.

Charlotte lifted her head, wiping at her mouth. "Did you hear that?"

Greg sat up on his elbows. "Oh, come on, it's probably just Frank shooting at something in the woods."

"That's what I'm afraid of!"

Sighing, Greg fixed himself, tucked his retiring wet cock back into his shorts. "I'm gonna' kill that guy!"

Outside the tent, Greg stared into the night. "Char, give me that flashlight, I can't see shit out here."

Digging through her gear, she pushed aside the tent flap, brought out the blue plastic shaft, snapped its light on. "Here."

Taking it, Greg wedged open the night, falling back into Charlotte with a cry a moment later when the beam fell on a naked figure, screams of horror ringing from the throat. "Frank—Charlotte, grab a blanket!"

Drinking in the air, Frank fought to stand, leaning over, his hands cuffing his knees. "I saw … I … saw it."

Throwing a blanket over him, Charlotte covered his body while Greg put the light in his face. "What happened—what did you see? Where's Melissa?"

At the the sound of her name, Frank weeped like a child, tears glossing his face, his voice cracked. "Dead, man—something big—she's fucking dead!"

Charlotte looked on Greg, her own eyes welling.

"This better not be a fucking joke, man—"

Frank grabbed him, pulled him close, his eyes wild and haunted. "IT'S NOT A FUCKING JOKE! I SAW IT MAN—A FUCKING MONSTER! FUCKING ATE MELISSA!"

Knocking his hands away, Greg staggered back, confident that Frank was pulling his leg. "A monster? Now I know you're messing—"

"We have to get out of here!" Frank screamed.

And before Greg or Charlotte could flick a tongue at his sudden dismissal, Frank dashed off into the woods, a white blur swallowed by the shadows between the pines.

Greg followed after him with the beam. "*Frank!*"

Charlotte shivered, and it was not the wind blowing from the lake, but of a tremendous pain —the pain of fear. And that fear wound along her mind until each finger and toe and limb and tooth shuddered with the involuntary reaction of the mind confounded by the unknown. But all was quickly revealed and educated when her eyes fell upon the grim tower of black hair and strength clotted in blood that reflected with awful clarity in the moonlight. Even in a mind of knowledge, one could scarcely describe with a sane eye the thing that stood in contemplative silence at the vague rim of light cast by a nest of coals and failing flames.

As a totem, it loomed, and in that black hairy face, a pair of the most demon inspired eyes tore a hole in the night with a red that burned bright as evening suns.

"Charlotte, what the fuck are you doing, come on!"

But then Greg saw what her eyes held, and he felt his mind weaken and a tremor worked up his body. He felt a scream in his throat and shouted for Charlotte. "Babe, run!"

Shaken from a spell, she turned and saw Greg, a crouching and broken-minded man shielded behind a thick pine.

Bound by a morbid curiosity, she turned back and faced those eyes that inflamed as the claws sprung out a fan of black hooks, bracketing her head.

Instantly, her hands flung up and plunged beneath the thick coat of hair that layered its arms and obscenely lengthened fingers. Unable to relieve the pressure which clamped onto her like a cuff of steel, she kicked and floundered at the beast, but her efforts proved ineffective and she screamed with futility.

Driving its reddened talons into her skull, Charlotte choked on grunts that issued up her throat behind a weltering of blood as her head broke like glass between its palms. Her body flopped and heaved.

The monster's roar rippled the lake as its back tensed and Charlotte burst apart in an explosion of bloody rags and meat that showered the woods.

"*Charlotte!*" Greg looked on in disbelief as chaos found his mind and compelled his feet to run—to run aimlessly into the black woods.

Blind, he ran, a flickering image in the woods chased by the shafts of moonlight, and on his trail, the bellowing crash of un-human vocals.

Miles had passed beneath his soles, the sweat of panic and fear beaded his face. Moonlight filtered past the needles, yet his eyes failed to absolve the black which swam around him, enfolding him into a nightmare of suggestion.

Something moved behind him, and he felt the eyes of a concealed invader. Staring unblinking into the dense black wall that restricted depth, he thought maybe something had detached itself from those immense and layering shadows; thought he spotted the swinging arms of some primitive ape high up in the trees, wondered why those same trees were shaking as though a wind were caught up there. He looked skyward, star points of light in his eyes, something black and solid as a mountain boulder descended over him with a strident shriek that liberated his own mounting terror to empty his lungs dry in a terrible volume that filled the woods.

Braced beneath the heels of feet too big and wide, Greg lay broken and ruined and splattered like a bug smeared on a windshield. The mighty beast roared up into the pines and beat at its chest as it surveyed with those burning eyes, the mutilated heap of gore clogging its toes.

CHAPTER 12

Ranger Rundell had decided to blow some steam and head out on patrol. It was the owner—that Pete fella'. Got under his skin like a bad case of psoriasis. But it was more than that. Something about the way his fat finger waved in his face, and the sheriff's face, had put his blood to dangerous levels, much like the sheriff's he suspected.

Driving on, his wheels sank and cracked over ruts, his headlights punched a hole in the dark. He managed to divert his bumper from some curious doe which gave him a startle rounding a bend.

Lowering his window, he rested his elbow on the frame. Thumbing at the lighter in his dashboard, he plugged a smoke between his lips. While waiting, he looked on the sky, noticed the moon up there, high and burning amidst a field of constellations. He thought about Caudel—thought about Wilmont. He wondered what had taken hold of the sheriff back in the office. It still bothered his mind thinking about what ailed the man. The way he sort of fell back against the wall, as though he were unaware of his own mind and place. It was scary, got Rundell to thinking about his mortality and all those ailments that hamper an old man; the incontinence, the loss of faculties and thoughts— all those gifts age bestows on to old bones and memories.

The lighter popped. He grabbed it, put its heated coil to the bushy end of his smoke. Inhaling deep, he replaced the lighter, blew out a cloud which was quickly grabbed and hurled out the window. "That won't happen to me," he told himself. "Old age issues. It's because Caudel don't take care of himself. That's what it is—that's all it is."

A while back, he passed the summer camp, spotted a pit of flames, saw the children and counselors ringed around its glow, sitting beneath the stars. *Probably telling ghost stories*, he told himself at the time.

But it was sheriff Caudel and Wilmont that gave him pause. He pulled his rig to the side of the road, put his window down, questioned them as to the purpose of their presence.

Caudel had explained to him that they weren't allowing the fat sonofabitch to dictate orders in his town. Said if he was unable to set foot on the property, wasn't nothing keeping him from patrolling its exterior.

Rundell laughed at that, complimented the sheriff, told him he was one crazy sonofabitch himself, and that he respected his decision to take matters into his own hands, but cautioned him against being observed by the counselors. It could spell disaster. Wilmont on the other hand he looked on curiously, asked him why he looked so sullen and asked him if there was anything he could offer the two. But Wilmont only shook his head, said he was following orders, and gave Rundell a look like maybe he was thinking the sheriff was off his rock.

Thinking back on it, Rundell wondered if that were true. With the episode in his office, he started to worry—especially considering Caudel was walking that camp with a shotgun in his arms. Made him shiver a bit.

But, ultimately, he dismissed the notion, carried on and wished the both of them good luck.

Now, his mind back on the road, he wound down a pass, his headlights spotting a structure ahead. Closer, he saw that it was a camper—or something that looked like a camper. He eased his speed, came to a rolling stop.

"I should probably check on them," he said.

Putting his gear in park, shutting the rig down, he stepped outside. The heat was still in the road and he felt it climbing up his shirt. His flashlight came on, breaking away the night. He puts its beam on the driver-side window of the camper, peeked inside, shrugged when nothing caught his eye. Going round back, he knuckled at the door a few rounds. "Hello? Anybody in there?"

Silence.

Trying the handle, he was met with a lock.

Turning away, he started back to his truck.

Throwing open the door, he felt the urge to turn and that's when his heart had about leapt out of his chest as something white limbed came winging out of the woods with a scream that put bumps up his back.

"HELP! OH PLEASE HELP ME!"

Instantly, Rundell went for his pistol, but hesitated after noticing the figure was a naked man, coated in a oily sheet of sweat. Now, Rundell had seen some things during his career as a ranger, but nothing so bizarre as a man disgorging from the black woods with his pecker slinging against his thighs.

"What—what the hell happened to you? Where are your clothes?"

"YOU HAVE TO GET ME OUT OF HERE MAN!"

"Calm down, sir, what—"

"I CAN'T CALM DOWN! PLEASE—WE HAVE TO LEAVE—NOW!"

Rundell figured there was no arguing with the man, instead, he helped him into the truck, handed him a blanket.

"Before we head out, tell me what the hell happened to you."

The man's eyes jumped around his skull. Nervously, he checked the woods thinking maybe something had followed him.

"My friends," he said. "They're all dead. ALL OF THEM!"

"Relax, relax, what happened exactly? What's your name—can you tell me your name?"

The man forced air into his lungs. "Frank—my name is Frank."

"Okay Frank, give me the story, what happened?"

"We don't have time—we have to go, now! It was right behind me—I heard it!"

Rundell gassed up the engine, put the truck in gear and headed back up to the station. "You're going to have to tell me something Frank."

"It was big …"

"What was?"

"Black … just covered in hair, black hair."

"A bear?"

"No … not a bear, but … I dunno," Frank looked ahead into the highlighted road. "It had big teeth, ate my girlfriend—swallowed her—just like that—fucking swallowed her!"

Rundell kept his eyes on both the road and the man. Took him a minute to drink that one in. "*Ate* your girlfriend?"

"Yeah, and my friends, fucking killed both of them. I thought I heard Charlotte scream, but I *heard* Greg; I heard his screams somewhere close to me in the woods."

"I'm going to bring you up to my station, I'll get you some help."

Rundell reached forward, grabbed the radio. "Sheriff Caudel, Rundell here—deputy Wilmont, do you read?"

There was a space of time before the radio crackled. "This is Wilmont, what is it Rundell?"

"Uh—I have a man here, found him on the road a couple of miles south from the camp—" he looked over to the shaking, frightened form "—you ain't going to believe this one."

Caudel came on the line. "What is this—Rundell, what's going on?"

"Man here says that something big killed his friends—something black and hairy."

The other end went silent.

"Sheriff?"

"Wilmont here—sheriff wants to know your location."

"Tell him I'm almost back to the station, I'm just passing the camp."

"Copy, we're rounding the back of Starlight. Sheriff says we'll we'll be there in five."

"Copy that."

Rundell looked over at that man. "Sure this was no bear or something? Supposedly there's an angry bear loose in these woods."

Frank put his eyes on the ranger, and in a deadpan voice said, "No … wasn't no fucking bear … no bear at all."

CHAPTER 13

On arrival, Caudel was the first in the door, his shotgun limp at his side, eyes poking from beneath his stetson. Sweat beaded on his face.

Rundell stood from behind his desk, put his hand out. "Right here, sheriff."

Caudel moved ahead, saw a blanketed, hunched form, seated, a cup of coffee in his hands. Laying his shotgun on the surface of an empty desk, Caudel stood over the man, knocked his hat back up on his head a notch. He recognized the face instantly; it was one of the hikers he had warned earlier in the day. "What's your name?"

The man looked up, trauma in his face, hands shaking, lips quivering. "F-F-Frank."

"Well, Frank, Rundell says you ran into something awful out there in the woods—this true?"

Wilmont walked up, sat on the edge of a desk, rifle resting over his lap. He relieved the hat on his head, placing it beside him; nodded to Rundell.

Frank swallowed down a gulp of black and sugar, his face paling. "Yes … it was horrible."

"Mind telling me exactly what happened out there?"

"I—I don't think I can."

"Of course you can. We're here to help you. But I need to know what you saw first."

Frank stared off at the wall, thoughts forming shapes in his head. Bad shapes, big black and nightmare shapes with blood stained fangs like a row of kitchen knives stained red and dripping black claws and flanks of meat in its fur and blood mottled and oily down its chest. "It … was a … it was a big, hairy thing … it was hairy all over …"

"What else?" Caudel pressed him, urging him to keep that memory intact.

Screams rang in his head, the eyes of sun-fire on his trail, bulky black arms snapping pines from its path like pencils. "It was tall—real tall."

"Tall like a man?"

"Taller!" Frank shouted, catching his voice. "Much taller than a man."

Wilmont shuffled from the desk, poured himself a cup of coffee. "Was it a bear, sir? Is that what you saw?"

Caudel looked on his deputy. "Not now deputy."

"It has to be a bear, what else could it be sheriff? Bigfoot?" Wilmont asked this with an annoyance that was palpable with each word.

"It wasn't a bear," Frank said with the assurance of knowing that what imprinted his pupils was something that bears and other things ran screaming away from. "Not a bear at all—

something bigger, something …" Tears broke down his face. "My girlfriend—Melissa—oh god … it fucking ate her."

Wilmont dropped a sugar cube in his cup, his eyebrow lifted. "The bear *ate* your girlfriend—"

Frank shot up on his feet, the blanket falling loose off his naked body, his eyes wild and red veined. "*It wasn't a fucking bear!*"

Caudel put a hand on Frank's shoulder. Rundell scooped up the blanket and covered the man.

"Take it easy," Caudel told him. "Sit back down here and tell me what it was, son. Don't be afraid to explain what you saw. I believe you when you say it wasn't a bear. I've seen it too." Frank looked up, as did Wilmont and Rundell.

"Sheriff?" Wilmont asked, still a bit incredulous and annoyed with the man.

"You've seen it too?" Frank asked, a feeling of companionship in his eyes.

Caudel nodded, leaning back. "Long time ago boy. But I need you to tell me—go on."

Wilmont continued to stir his coffee, Rundell leaned against the wall, the clock overhead ticking lightly, the windows opened in the place pulled in the chatter of crickets.

"I was … I was with my girlfriend—Melissa. And we were together—down by the lake. It was real dark out there and Melissa said … said she heard something—something like footsteps around us. I didn't believe her, then something was standing there—like right next to us. It was big, black, almost like the shadow of some large tree that you can't see all that well. But then its eyes opened—"

"Like balls of red fire?"

Frank looked up to Caudel, tears lining his face. "You *have* seen it?"

Caudel nodded. "Yes. Yes, son I have."

Wilmont set his coffee down, anger in his voice. "Sheriff, what the hell is going on here—what is this shit? Ain't nothing more than a bear out there in those woods Caudel; the grizzly from last year— that's all it is! This man here—" he pointed to Frank "—is clearly mistaken by what he'd seen. People see shit in the dark, and what he saw was a bear, but scared as he is, his mind was showing him anything else besides a damn bear!"

"Deputy, I advise you take a seat and relax—"

"Relax? I can't relax, Caudel! You've been driving me mad all day with your manner and the blatant dodging of my questions. I know something is on that mind of yours and for some damn reason you feel it in your heart not to enlighten me with these things. So what the fuck is going on here sheriff? No more games! What is it? What is this animal!"

Caudel maintained his composure, not allowing anger to circumvent his calm. Instead, he sat back, put a hand on the young man's shoulder, urged him to rest.

Frank sat back, his eyes staked on the sheriff.

"I've been quiet too long," Caudel started. "But what I'm about to tell you is the God honest truth deputy. I remember it like it was only the day before. And each night I wake up sweating, I swear to you and the lord above that I can still hear that thing in the night, and see those eyes looking in on me from outside my window."

Rundell stood silent, his eyes jumping from Wilmont to Caudel, uneasy about the tension palling his office.

"It was twenty years ago …"

CHAPTER 14

Deputy Roy Caudel
1967

After what the boy told me, I had trouble believing much of anything he related in grim detail. I thought the young man was delirious, maybe running a fever, but that didn't account for the blood on his body and those furtive glances in his eyes.

We were nearing the town when a great big pine tree laid itself across the road. I remember being aggravated by that tree and told the boy I'd return in a moment, after I figured a way to remove that big tree, or find a path around it. He grabbed a hold of my wrist, told me not to leave him; told me that tree was put their by that demon as a trap. I merely assured the boy it was the work of nature and nothing on this planet had placed that there with ill intention.

It was when I was outside, the rain started pecking at my hat, dotting my back, adding to the mud under my boots. A wind blew down from the mountain and I remember it being cold. Confused as I was, staring down at the tree, a sound busted the patter of rain and shook my nerves raw. It was a scream like I'd never heard in my life; even during the war I hadn't never heard a man scream like that. But it was made worse because that racket was from a boy's lungs and not a man.

I turned back, my eyes caught sight of something in the woods. That's when I saw that black shape in the woods, and that kid pinned beneath its arm, screaming and kicking and crying.

I'm thinking it was a man, so instantly, I went for my truck, tried the radio but couldn't get through. Think it had something to do with the storm still boiling over the area. Anyway, I grabbed my rifle from the rack and headed up that mountain, on the trail of those screams that were becoming more distant the further I pressed on.

I'd gone maybe a mile or so when the woods got thick and elevation leveled out. So thick in places I wondered if I'd be able to shoulder my rifle at some charging predator in time. I remembered pulling my pistol and my boots all but sinking in a bed of pine needles. All around that land was a lush carpet of wet needles and rough columned pines and hemlock, the branches so thick above in places that I had a natural shield to the rain.

I judged that I was working up and down several slopes and wondered if I'd be able to find my way back to the rig. But I couldn't stop and think about that, because out there, in that misty screen that hung in the woods, I could still hear them screams.

I knew I'd been gone a while, determined by that sky overhead that was shaded more a bruise than gray. I vaguely remember worrying about lightning coming down on top of me.

Anyway, I noticed the trees starting to thin out around me and ahead of me, and something about the way those pines started clearing made me wonder if this was the work of axe blades and hardened bodies, a cultivated land. My thoughts about it were confirmed after I spotted what looked to be huts and structures of a sorts, centered amidst a wall of thick woods at the foot of the mountain.

I holstered my piece and brought the rifle up. I listened out for those screams but wasn't hearing much of anything but the rainfall spattering the earth.

As I neared what looked to be some old camp of sorts, my eyes were welcomed to a motley collection of thatch roofed dwellings, and an honest-to-God tepee centered in that gathering.

But something grabbed my heart and gave it a good squeeze. It was the bodies, strewn about like they were, like driftwood scattered on a beach after a storm. Most were beyond simple description, some were nothing but torsos and headless things, pieces and strips looped on branches and crammed high up in the trees;

others broken open, their insides scooped clean, rainwater pooling their cavities red. There wasn't much blood on the ground because of the rain I suspected. In a quick estimation, there had to be a couple of dozen if not more of these folks, I couldn't be certain on account of the destruction to the bodies was appalling and the work of an evil mind.

I thought of the boy and wondered where he could be. I felt my knees go weak as the revelation of what he related to me back in the truck had some truth in it. These people—these Indians—had been slaughtered. And let me tell you, this wasn't the work of men with rifles or common tools, but of something pernicious. It was like a hurricane of sword blades and hatchets and butcher knives and iron headed mallets came sweeping through the place, catching everything living in a whirlpool of wrath, giving it a shake and disgorging what was left in a blowing explosion of mutilated madness that splashed over the land in a grisly net.

I took a moment to collect myself, and even to this day those bodies spring up out at me in my head and behind my eyes in the most un-welcomed moments.

As I walked on ahead, checking the huts and structures for survivors, picking around emptied skulls and contorted bodies, the heaped wreckage of human offal and rubbery things and what looked suspiciously like limbs that had been gnawed thin by a set of big teeth, I reckoned nothing was left breathing. But then I heard a sound, and turned immediately to that sound, thinking some horror had waited for me to turn my back to it and come to wrap me in its arms.

But instead, it was a man, limping, a ragged hole where an arm used to be. A thick flap of skin hung off his chin and most of the flesh around his mouth looked as though a knife had carved it away. I thought he was grinning at me with those blood stained teeth of his, but without lips, that skeletal grin was a perpetual thing, and I felt pity for the man. He fell to the ground, reached a hand out, started speaking in some broken dialect—and let me tell you now, a man speaking with no lips and most of his face scraped raw from the bone, was a most hideous and loathsome sound, like a corpse trying to communicate.

I crouched near him, told him I was looking for a boy that was taken by some big black bodied thing, like a tall man—a strong man able to carry a body away like it had. Then I asked him what happened to himself and these people.

His eyes grew real wide like I thought the both of them would roll out of his skull. That skeletal jaw started chattering again and he told me in this forced and busted English that took a lot of effort on my end to understand, that he saw it come through there, carrying that boy, and the boy was screaming under its arm. And then he pointed a shaking finger to the woods so I reckoned thats where that thing had taken the boy.

I figured the man was practically dead so I started towards those woods and he grabbed me around the ankle, telling me it was a demon from the mountain. And like the boy, he carried on about its origins from the stars and how the lightning was not lightning at all, but a means of conveyance for the demon. It made not a lick of sense, and like the boy, I believed this man to be delusional and shattered of mind, things of that nature. The man kept pointing to the mountain, muttering things in that primitive dialect of his, then his eyes grew wide in his skull and his heart must of burst because he laid there on the earth, dead, rain beading on his face. I stood there in some sort of suspension, staring at that finger which was locked rigid pointing at the mountain.

I remember looking up at the ridge and wondered just what in the hell he was actually pointing at. The mountains or the sky? It was hard to say.

Figuring I'd lost the boy, I backed out of that graveyard, and started to turn, when the most execrable peal of a scream sent a wave of rancid heat over me, and I turned as though something had physically grabbed me and swung me around.

I shudder to think about what I saw. It hurts my tongue in ways you'll never understand. But I saw it. Goddamnit, I saw that thing. Staring at me with those eyes that I swear to you were not eyes at all, but two pits of liquid red. A face mind you, of coarse, black fur and a mouth crammed with fangs longer and thicker than my own fingers. It was colossal. A wall of steel that I wondered if my own rifle could harm. I felt an instant disdain and loathsome hate and fear of the thing and felt my heart screaming at me to run. I saw what was in one of those immense claws, and that was the straw that had me running blind down that mountain, screaming, thinking it was right behind me the whole time, just teasing me. I knew it could catch me—God, I knew it could if it wanted to do it. Because that thing was not natural, no sir, that thing was not of this goddamn planet. But if I was to describe it in terms to justify what I was seeing, I would say it shared the same primal outline and massive breast, long broad arms, squat in the legs, yet the powerful and long frame of a jungle primate. An antithesis of nature, the genesis of some malignant womb.

I managed to fight my way through the dark woods and must have covered miles, but I finally came back out on the road, and saw my truck sitting there, the door still open and rain still falling. I hurried down the muddy slope and jumped inside, fired the engine and tore over that trunk and damn near went off several cliffs until I was back in town, still thinking about that mangled, butchered slosh of meat in its fist, and I knew it was that boy.

CHAPTER 15

Camp Starlight
1987

It stood there, just between the trees, an oblong block of shadow diverging from the natural configuration of the woods. If one were to glance closely to the conflicting oddity that gapped the uniformity of the pines, perception would divulge the red spheres of its eyes and perhaps the dilated grin on its black face. But none chanced the woods at such an hour to explore the vast black shadows that drank the color and confiscated the beauty and replaced its allure with rooted fears and the revulsion of dark and empty spaces and what haunts and lurks in such gulfs where light is revoked.

It had leered at the migration of the children to the cabins. Only a select group had remained beneath the stars, encircled around a pit of flames. And it was that point of fire that its eyes perceived high up on the ridge that sat just above the camp, and the figures which where sharp in aspect by those flames, that drew its bulk from the ridge to glide seamlessly down the ramps and shelves of rock and pines, hunger pooling its mouth.

Divorced from the shadows into the mottled flecks of moonlight, it approximated itself to a dark structure in which the rushing sounds of blood reached its ears. The sounds of hearts in rest and minds catapulted to distant lands of mystery and illusion—the dreams of children.

Tracing the seam of a window, its talon scratched the glass.

Ron checked his watch for the third time that night. "Ten more minutes and I can get some rest."

The night was warm, but the wind blowing down off the mountain had a pinch to it. It was quiet out there, all around him, except for that wind brushing through the woods, he would have thought he were alone out there. *That would be something*, he thought. *Just me and this flashlight walking this camp alone, that moon following my every step and a wind to play at my mind and make me think all kinds of spooky things are lurking just out of sight.*

But Ron was not alone at the camp—something he had to keep telling himself. But at that moment, it was just him and that flashlight, no other counselor or camper to share a conversation with, he felt the isolation of the place getting to him. Never timid; not one to jump at things going snap in the dark, but something about these woods was putting the hairs on his neck a bit too straight for his liking.

Ron couldn't explain to you this feeling. Not even if you approached him and asked him what it was that had him checking those pockets of shadow that filled between the trees so often, or why he had that funny look in his eye each time he stared up at the mountain that poked at that sky bursting with so many stars.

Maybe it was the scare about that animal the sheriff was losing his head about earlier. "Nah, that guy was just a loony," he said to himself.

Luckily Ron had drawn the early shift tonight. He sure didn't feel like getting up in the middle of the night for a late watch, walking this place even later than it was now.

"Sure could use some coffee right about now," he said. It was a good idea. In fact, it was the right idea. So Ron started heading towards the lodge, and he still had that light sweeping holes in the dark.

His hand reached out to grab the door, and something stopped him cold.

It was a scream—or something that sounded like a scream. It was hard to determine with the wind in his ears.

Turning, he faced the lake, looked on the cabins which sat squat and black beneath the pines. Tensing, he started forward, and this time he did hear a scream.

"Jesus …"

Ron increased his pace back to the cabins, thinking maybe somebody was messing around and doing what campers are known to do—playing gags and tricks and such.

The flashlight beam bounced over the pine coated ground in front of him, and again he paused —paused because now there was more than just one scream, but what sounded like many screams, and all those screams were coming together and maximizing into a pitch that was scraping at his spine.

Pushing the light into the woods, he saw a figure coming at him.

"*Ron!*"

It was Brittney, at least, he thought it was Brittney.

"Ron!"

"Brittney?"

"The kids—the boy's cabin—over there!"

He followed her finger. "I don't see anything— Brittney, where you going?"

Brittney had off run towards the cabin she was pointing at.

"Wait!"

Damnit.

Catching up, he asked her, "What is it? What's going on? Is this a joke?"

Without looking him at him, she said, "Ron, I saw it, I saw it!" And there was nothing funny about that voice.

Ron felt his knees quiver after they reached

the cabin and something inside that cabin gave his heart a few skips. It was a sound that opened parts of the mind that remained locked for reasons that were important to maintain sanity. It was the sound of children, or sheep; something young and fresh to this world being mauled and chewed on; having their bodies violated with teeth and nails and ripped open and emptied over gaping spiked chasms to feed a belly that was never satisfied.

Ron could almost picture the blood bursting along the seams of the cabin; blowing out the windows in a red torrent.

Brittney had her hand covering her mouth, and tears fell over her fingers, a moan trembled up her throat.

Ron felt like running away, and even thought about how far he'd get if he started right now and turned away from that sickening noise that was getting to be too much right then.

Footsteps behind him caused his heart to leap and he turned and almost screamed at the figures coming towards him in the night.

"What is that—what the fuck is going on?" It was Marcus.

Angela, Julie, and Jake were gathered around him, sleep still in their eyes.

"Oh God, I saw it—I saw it go into that cabin," Brittney stammered but said nothing more.

Marcus was about to question her, but after getting a look at the cabin, seeing that big ragged hole torn through the siding, his throat had dried up.

"We have to do something!" Brittney screamed.

But nobody wanted to get near that cabin.

Jake started forward, but hesitated after what sounded like something that could not be.

A monster.

And that's exactly the only description his mind was allowing him to conceive. There was no alternative, no justification that would lead him otherwise. It sounded like something out of a nightmare; something that chased you down empty black corridors or through moonlit graveyards; haunted you in the bone heaped burrows of catacombs or peaked out at you from inside the closet with one juicy red eye.

"I can't go in there—I can't do it!"

None of them could, and none of them had offered to. Instead, they stood as solitary mutes beneath the pines, staring at that gaping black hole blown in the side of the cabin, and could only cry in their throats at the horrible screams that were cut silent by pulpy, twisting wet sounds and splashes of what sounded like water hitting the ground.

"Somebody get on the radio, we have to reach the sheriff!"

But nobody could turn away; their minds had been ruptured; a paralysis that held them hostage to that spot as grim voyeurs to a bloodbath.

Brittney backed away a few steps and found the courage to show her back to that cabin and ran screaming to the lodge, to the radio.

CHAPTER 16

Deputy Wilmont hadn't blinked once during the story. In fact, he was almost certain he hadn't breathed. Did he believe the sheriff? If you had queried him with such a question right then, he would likely put his eyes into your own and question *you* as to the validity of your ears.

Yes, he believed the sheriff. Why? Because all his life he had known Roy Caudel, and he known the man to be an honest and God fearing man—like much of the townsfolk who populated Starbright Springs.

But Roy was different. Where folks may tell a simple lie or smack off an exaggeration over a round of beers, Wilmont had never known Caudel to once convolute his words or act imprudently, not only with the badge pinned to his chest, but during his personal time.

All day Wilmont had suspected things about the sheriff, but this was something else. It was in opposition to each feeling and suspicion he had of the man. Caudel never once let his nerves get raw from the bear attack last year, but this … this *beast*, it laid open something inside his heart. And to think the sheriff had been carrying this horror in his head for that length of time with not once coming forward and saying, *look Wilmont, I gotta' get something off my chest*. Nope, he took that pain and held on to it and it haunted him all his days.

"I don't know what to say, sheriff—I'm sorry. I feel like such a fool."

Caudel nodded. "Don't be. Who would believe such a crazy yarn anyhow?"

It was like Caudel had read the thoughts in his head.

"I just can't imagine living with something like that; something so ... heart stressing. And how you never told a soul to relieve that pressure. I don't think I'll ever understand."

"I wanted to—God how I wanted to get that off my chest for so long. But it's not a common thing to speak about and have people believe your words, because, what are you going to say? '*I saw a monster in the woods and it took a kid up the mountain*'. I couldn't even bring myself to tell the sheriff at the time. He was a good man too, by the name of Shupe. But he was a different breed from you and I, he would never a believe a wild-eyed deputy as myself, explaining to him that I'd seen bodies out in those woods and a society and all that— he would have looked on me like I had smoked something funny."

"What did you do after that—I mean how—"

"If you're asking did I go back up that mountain

and check on things? Well, yeah, I did. I told Shupe that I was headed back out to the forest roads on account I was concerned about folks being stranded in the storm. He looked over his newspaper at me and told me ain't nobody stupid enough to be up on that mountain at this time; told me to punch out and go enjoy some beers. So I punched out, went home, and grabbed me a shotgun and headed back up that mountain. I saw that tree still lying there in a pool of mud and left my truck on the road and went up into those woods, and I toiled those slopes with a flashlight and shotgun in my arms. I eventually found my way back to that settlement and there was nothing left. No bodies, no blood, nothing but a ghost town and matchsticks where there were once structures. I heard something up on the mountain above me, like something climbing up there, and … well, I lost my nerve. I left and never turned back and I haven't been back there since. I couldn't face it deputy. I just couldn't face it."

"I'm sorry, Roy."

Ranger Rundell looked ashen. "I can't believe something like that—I mean I believe you sheriff, but … that's hard to believe, you know?"

Caudel fixed him with a stare. "I know all too well. But what we got to do now is get to that camp, because, call it intuition or a gift from God, but I feel that thing is close, maybe too close … I feel it in my bones gentlemen."

Frank hadn't said a word or made a sound. He

was just sitting there with that empty cup of coffee in his hands pulling from it like it was still full. He was rocking back and forth and something about his eyes had Caudel thinking the man was broken.

The radio crackled. "*Help!*"

It was a channel that came in spotty but clear enough to hear. Rundell scooped up the receiver. "Hello? Who is this?"

"—camp—Brittney—please—us!"

"This is ranger Rundell. Is this Starlight?"

"—Star—Brittney—help!"

Caudel and Wilmont looked at one another.

Caudel was on his feet, Wilmont beside him. "Rundell, grab a rifle from that cabinet over there —deputy, you brought along enough ammo I hope?"

Wilmont padded his bulging pockets. "Plenty sheriff."

Caudel laid a hand on Frank. "Frank, you sit tight, we'll be back for you soon and get you some help."

Frank continued rocking and muttering things, drinking from that empty cup.

Equipped, the three of them charged out of the office. Caudel raced to his rig, Wilmont on his tail, the sound of gear rattling in their pockets and hands was the only sound in that black night.

The engine fired loud and the wheels scratched the road, sending up plumes of dust and pine needles. Rundell followed close behind, both vehicles just two pinpoints of red light growing dim on a dust choked road.

CHAPTER 17

Once she reached what she thought was the ranger station, Brittney hurried back outside, thinking everything would be okay, or perhaps passed. It was a mistake, because at the moment she left those doors behind in the lodge, Jake came running up, blood on his face, in his hair. "It took Ron! It came out of the Cabin, took him and broke him open and started—started eating him! Right there—right there in front of us!"

Brittney had staggered back, feeling like she were about to crash to the ground in a faint.

"Did you hear me?" Jake shouted in her face, taking her shoulders in his hands and shaking them. "It ate Ron, ate him! Broke him apart!"

"The kids in the cabin—what about the kids in the cabin?" she shouted.

"*Dead!* All of them *dead!*"

Jake dropped his hold on her and went screaming madly into the night. She watched after him and noticed most of the cooking staff had joined him; a couple of small dots too which she recognized were kids.

Brittney felt her heart thrumming behind her eyes and then she started hearing screams and they were getting loud and she started glimpsing figures running around in the dark and she thought for one moment there was something like a blob of black shadow moving around out there between the trees, chasing those smaller figures.

Conditioned to help folks in need, Brittney ran forward, towards all those screams and she questioned herself if she were doing the right thing, because her mind and heart were urging her to run in the opposite way and don't look back.

Closer to the cabins now, the screams were wild, some were cut away and others were shrill.

A kid ran up to her out of the dark, startling her with a pale face striped in blood. "It's a monster, it's a monster!"

Brittney grabbed the kid and shook her. "A monster? Where is it?"

"It's eating the campers. I saw it eating the campers—"

Then like Jake, the little girl started running away and screaming, her hands above her head, the back of her nightgown splashed in red.

The camp had devolved into chaos.

As she ran forward in some frivolous attempt to make sense of things and lend a hand, she started picking out the lumps of things that had once been campers; all of which were hammered down into grisly smears and opened up in unnatural ways, their insides on the outside and strung around their bodies as though something thought it would be funny to play with all those sinewy red ropes and scatter blood around like toddlers tossing paint.

A group of kids came running up to her, their faces back to the woods, ever fearful of some nightmare just behind them.

"Brittney!" one of the kids said, reaching a hand out. "Help us! It's eating the counselors and campers—"

She shouted at them to run away but they had already passed her and she was screaming at herself.

"Brittney!" It was Julie's voice. "Brittney over here!"

Brittney followed that voice and saw Julie dragging something behind her.

"Help me Brittney!"

Crying in her throat, Brittney ran over to Julie and when she saw what it was that she was dragging behind her, Brittney coughed out a chunk of dinner that stumbled down her shirt.

"It got her Brittney—it came out of that cabin and just pulled her head right off and swallowed it!"

Brittney held her stomach and blew some vomit from her mouth.

"I gotta' get Angela to the doctor Brittney, she needs help—she needs it bad!"

Brittney stared in disbelief as Julie just pushed on by her, dragging a headless Angela behind her, blood thick and smeared, trailing a long band of clotted red in her path.

Feeling like she should just turn and run, Brittney felt her mind closing in on her. Felt her body starting to collapse. It was all so much. It was a horror show, something you only saw on those big screens like when she was back home and Joe, her boyfriend, would take her to see these awful blood soaked films and point out to her how this is destined to be a classic. Films that had monsters eating folks beneath the sea, or rising up out of the earth with their faces crawling in worms, or a man dressed in denim, a drill in his hands, coring skulls and breasts.

A shout of screams brought her back from her head, and she saw something that dropped her to her knees.

It was right there, right in a spot of moonlight. An obscene thing. Something right out of those same movies. Something that ruined the mind once you looked at; made you rethink things such as the reality of ghoul packs hunting beneath tombstones; that scratching sound in your closet; that thing waiting for a foot to slip off the bed to pull you under; monsters and terrors ripped from the movies and placed right in front of you. She started screaming in her mind and released that scream from her mouth and her hands started shaking and tears crawled down her face.

If she were to imagine the haunter of the dark; the lurker in the woods; the monster in the attic;

the ogre of myth, eating babies and swallowing kids—that was it. Right there in front of her. And right then, that molten eyed beast—that *Ogre*—had a kid in its mouth like it was sucking down a knot of spaghetti.

She felt her knees hit the earth and she started wailing right there and saw the screaming campers running aimlessly around her.

The thing caught one crying boy in its mighty fist, brought the boy to its face and opened that mouth and took a bite out of the camper like a snack. Blood winged into its eyes yet it still ate and chewed until it was finished and tossed the kicking legs behind it into the woods.

It moved with a speed that took her eyes from her skull as she watched it race toward another group of straggling campers. It leaped into the air with a scream like a baboon and came down on top of them, pounding them down into a mutilated paste of blood and shattered bones, taking big red bites out of several. It took a couple of them in its fist and just held those screaming youth's over its mouth and swallowed them down whole. Brittney saw the eyes in those faces roll white as they sank beneath a cavern of blood and reddened fangs.

A few decided to crawl away while it was feeding, crying for their mommies and daddies, but the ogre caught wind of their escape and scooped up those campers and started pulling their arms and legs from their bodies like a kid plucking wings off a butterfly.

Brittney went prone in the pine needles, reaching a hand out and screaming and vomiting and wanting to help but knowing there was not a damn thing she could do about it. She felt her mind shutting down after watching the ogre crunch those limbs in its mouth and tossing the screaming torsos over its back where they landed with the most hideous of wet thumps.

"Brittney!"

Her eyes started flashing, and she turned and saw Marcus, he was running up on her, moonlight and blood on his body.

"Brittney, come on I got you," he said as he wrapped those thick strong arms around her and lifted her from the ground, carrying her away from that feeding thing.

But the Ogre felt something, and it came forward like an ape charging out of the jungle and threw its weight against the evading couple. Marcus lost his balance and let go of Brittney whose body sprung from his arms and landed hard with a grunt.

Instantly, Marcus was on his feet, shouting at Brittney. "Brittney, get the hell out of here—now!"

Brittney had so many emotions running through her mind it was starting to clog her senses. She looked on Marcus like some sort of hero right then, something she would have never equated with the man. He was standing there, facing that anthropomorphic monstrosity and throwing his arms up at it, screaming and shouting.

And maybe if this was a movie she might have laughed and blinked an eye at the absurdity of it all. But this was real, something that she was still having trouble believing, even after all that she had seen in a space of what could only have been minutes.

"Marcus—run!"

But Marcus wasn't listening; too busy throwing up a wall to that monster. The ape-like horror hit its chest with a fist larger than the head of the human barring its way.

Marcus shouted and screamed at it some more; put his arms in the air and waved them around as if he were repulsing a bear. But the ogre hadn't budged and now the strength Marcus felt was coming out of him and running down his leg in a hot stream as that big and ugly ape started for him and grabbed a hold of his body and lifted him to its face and its mouth fell open like a laundry shoot and those big sharp teeth sheared open his face and most of his throat out in a single bite that splashed a thick wave of blood and pieces of brain and teeth into that monster's black hair and face.

"MARCUS!"

Marcus shuddered in death and the ogre dropped the man; its foot crushing over the breast and spattering blood and cracking bone beneath its heel.

It was coming for her. Those red ovens heated and those fangs beading blood and all that red oily blood that looked black in the moonlight on its broad oval body came stomping itself over to her. Brittney screamed as it stood there, looming over her like some terrible mountain of flesh and blood, red drops splattering on her face and getting in her mouth and eyes.

Its hand opened up and those long fingers, like hideous barbed spider legs, settled over her and she screamed at the feel of the talons sinking into her hair and its breath blowing in her face.

But then something staggered her fear and the beast retreated back a step.

Suddenly, the air around her head was alive with the sound of whistling and anger; lead and all manner of explosions ripping around her and carving out holes in the monster's body that expelled a black blood that splashed down onto her face and soaked her hair and clothes.

Curled in a ball, Brittney chanced a look behind her and saw three dark figures and the flames licking from barrels and the sound of weapons discharging and brass flinging.

She fell on to her back and wormed toward the three and could feel the heat of those rounds whipping above her and smacking wet flesh beyond her.

A hand groped her arm, and she looked up into the face of the sheriff. "I got you—I got you sweety —"

But Caudel didn't have her, because all that firing and lead was like tossing pebbles against a brick wall. The thing lurched forward, black blood running down its body. It swung out a massive arm and Caudel caught the strength and went spinning back against his men in a pile.

The ogre grabbed Brittney and raced away, back into the woods, back towards the mountain.

CHAPTER 18

Caudel stared on and was joined by both Wilmont and Rundell, their weapons smoking in their hands, brass laying around them, screams of the dying and mutilated heaped and revealed by blades of moonlight skewering pines.

"Get up damnit, we have to go after it!"

Caudel raised himself from the pile, helped the deputy to his feet. He saw that look in Wilmont's eyes and knew exactly how he was feeling after having regarded that big black thing, but there was no time for standing around and questioning reality and maybe their sanity.

"Rundell, get the hell up, we have to go!"

But the ranger hadn't moved, he just laid there in the needles, a look of absolute dread clouding his eyes. "I can't, sheriff—I c-can't go after that thing."

Caudel and Wilmont helped the man up and shoved his rifle into his arms. "We need your help, Rundell, we don't have time for this."

Rundell felt his heart knotting up in his chest looking on those woods. "I ... can't, I can't do it."

Caudel wished he had the time to slap the man and bring some senses to him, but there was no time for such things. Instead, he used logic.

"Rundell," he said, stepping in front of him so the ranger's eyes looked into his own. "Wilmont and I are headed up that mountain. You go back to the truck, rally the town; you tell them their sheriff needs them and it is of the utmost importance they fall in line. You understand?"

Rundell nodded and swallowed, the memory of that thing looping behind his eyes.

"You tell them to get their biggest guns and grab all the medical equipment we have—get doc Billington too. You tell Margaret to reach out to every voice in the area and have them bring all the supplies they can carry and to hurry—Rundell, you listening to me?"

The ranger nodded, but his eyes were distant. "I just can't believe it—"

"We don't have time for this—you just do as I ordered you to, copy?"

Rundell's eyes came back into focus. "Yeah—yes, sheriff."

Before Rundell could counter with one of the many questions brimming his mind, Caudel and Wilmont were two vague blurs dimming in the woods.

She screamed and beat at the massive body with tiny fists, and drove her nails into the skin which layered its bulk in a coat of armor. Brittney cried and shook and all around her was a blur of woods that flashed into a solid band of black, and above her the stars shimmered and scattered the width of the sky, only blotting by the rising black hills which the beast covered with supple ease.

She glanced below and saw the woods as a black sea, the tops knitted into a mottled bed of spikes. For one brief moment, the beast had stopped, and Brittney cried and screamed in a wave that would alert ears in a radius of miles. Suddenly, the sky overhead had darkened and she saw walls enclosing around her and the beast; rough and hewed as if by tools and not nature. And somewhere ahead a faint gleam of strange light guided the beast. It was a cave, and Brittney screamed as the light gave distinction to that which it held.

CHAPTER 19

The moon sat at their backs and spotted their advance up the mountain. It had been hard going, and it was only with the addition of a ceaseless adrenaline had they persisted up that rocky incline; two shadowed figures armed and breathless.

Besides the labor of lungs, both were silent; thoughts loud in their minds.

It had seemed as hours had passed since their weapons rattled and the beast roared with each impact cloven of its body, but judging by the moon, no less than an hour had eclipsed that awful slaughter of the camp.

In the lead of the advance, Caudel stumbled and fought to retain his balance, but felt the dire restrictions of age upon his old bones, and the breath in his lungs thinning as the mountain tested both resolve and strength—two attributes which were fast on the decline.

But it was the images of those children in his eyes, in his mind. It was the mutilation and barbaric treatment of the corpses which sat in twisted bows and carpeted the red earth like wrappers scattered by winds. But it was no winds that hurled these wrappers of flesh and bone and blood, but of that foul and abhorrent anthropoid; that demon of coarse black hair and sickled talons and eyes that burned redly. The screams too, held their resolve, and it echoed about his skull in a resonation that grew to terrible timbres. Afflicted by such reflection, Caudel, a man of years, continued up that mountain with the confidence that had kept his heart strong and alive.

Wilmont came to a stop, his back heaving. "Sheriff—"

Caudel turned. "We don't have time, deputy."

"But, just—let me catch my breath."

Caudel drank in the mountain air, his shotgun heavy in his arms. "We're done here. Time to move."

Sighing, Wilmont fell in behind the sheriff and marveled at the endurance which still lingered in his bones.

On their race through the woods, Wilmont was burdened with doubt. It struck him with each step, and he worried they were running to their dooms. After all, each bullet and pellet that opened that monster had not altered its strength or strides, on the contrary, the thing moved like the wind, and its strength was that of no comparison.

In those woods, he braced for the creature to reach out from the shadows and grab them, break them down into puddles and toss their skins into the trees, but Caudel had shown no worries, and if he had any, it was not evident in his manner.

But Wilmont worried, worried as he was now on that slope of rock and moonlight. Each pool of shadow on that rocky redoubt held a pair of red eyes or the flinging grasp of black nails. He would never admit these fantastical shapes in his mind, for to do so would only add fuel to a mind flooded with forbidden horrors.

"Right there," Caudel whispered.

Wilmont kneeled beside the sheriff. "What is that?"

Caudel stared over his shotgun. "Looks like some sort of cave or tunnel of sorts."

"Sure is big, sheriff."

It was. A hole big enough to accommodate the width and height of a tank.

"I'm thinking right in there is where we're going to find this thing."

Wilmont had a good feeling they would run into that thing in there too, if not other things—things eager to manifest from his mind in hideous black, skulking shapes.

Caudel turned and looked out behind him; glared out and below him and to the stretching woods that sat like the petrified waves of a black sea. "We're higher than I imagined."

"You think Rundell is securing the cavalry, sheriff?"

"I imagine he came out of it during the drive down, I'm hoping we get some help soon."

"You really think the locals can help us with this one?"

Caudel padded lightly forward, the question in his mind. Did he think that a mob of citizens with rifles and shotguns and pistols—even a few machine-guns he was well aware of—could handle this monster and beat its body down into a sludging mass? He had to have faith that it was possible, because without that faith, then he was willing to bet that nothing on this earth would have the capacity to end that demon and dispel its plague on this land.

"I have to believe they can, deputy. Come on."

CHAPTER 20

At the mouth of the cave, they held into a copse of pine and shadow. "I'll lead," Caudel whispered.

Leading with his shotgun out ahead of him, he stepped lightly into the shaft. Keeping to the wall; to a thin layer of shadow, he felt his way gingerly and cautiously along the cold stone wall.

Wilmont on his heels, they both moved together, slowly swallowed whole by the blackness that drowned the cave.

"I can't see," Wilmont said.

"I ain't seeing much myself," Caudel agreed.

The moonlight sat behind them as a silver sheet at the mouth far beyond.

"I don't think it's wise to walk through here without some sort of light."

Caudel was scared too. Yes, he was scared. More scared than he had ever been in his life. More scared than when he was nearly buried beneath a rain of artillery or repulsed that human wave of madness and grim eyes and bayonets; more scared than the time that monster had that boy melting blood and organ meat over its fist, staring into his eyes with those red burning orbs. So Caudel understood that maybe Wilmont figured it would be best for them to cut their losses and get the fuck out of that cave and head back down that mountain and wait for more men and weapons to storm this fortress.

But he couldn't. Caudel could not bring himself to turn away from this and leave that poor girl behind, dead or alive. It was the guilt over the years of that boy springing up in his mind whenever it felt the need to. There were many times he felt like eating that service pistol of his and end those nightmares, but that was something Roy Caudel could never do. No sir, Roy Caudel was a man of God, and eating a bullet was tantamount to booking a flight to hell. So, he lived with it, and it ate him up and chewed on him for all these years and had yet to spit or shit him out.

Roy Caudel was not leaving that girl behind. And if Wilmont wanted to retreat, he would look at the man no different, because he understood that a man could only take so much before the mind splinters and ain't nothing left inside but a haunting echo.

"You can go back if you want."

Wilmont stopped. "I ain't leaving you sheriff."

Caudel faced his deputy but couldn't see him all that good. "I won't think any different of you if you turn away from here right now."

Deputy Wilmont knew that to be true, but abandoning Roy after what he'd seen and knew to be haunting this cave somewhere, was not something he could find himself living with.

"I'm with you sheriff—to the end."

They prodded on silently, and fearfully. Running into rounded pillars of stone that caused them to choke back screams, thinking they had stumbled into the beast.

They felt the ground slope gently away beneath their tread, and far down that wandering, broad black shaft was a dim point of light. A vague starburst of lambent, hazy jade.

"What's that?"

"I have no clue deputy, but I think we're on the right track."

Brittney tried to scream but found her voice was bound by silence. How? She couldn't know for sure, but it worked to mitigate her vocals into that of a piercing whisper. All around her the black was dispelled by that green light that bathed the walls jade. Her eyes searched the arched ceiling and jumped and shuddered in her sockets at the origin of that light. And in her mind, words came and went, yet descriptions failed to illustrate which she saw. She felt a cold wind from some vague recess and felt her body shiver—her naked body.

Curled at the foot of the creature, she desperately attempted to conceal her breasts and sex, but it mattered not because her hands were bound by a thick nest of cables. She looked pleadingly into that black demon face, but knew it had no compunction of morality or care, and was merely a tool in a grim design.

It came forward, emerging from behind the beast, a tall and slender figure of glittering purple scales and oval sockets pooled with a black liquid. Its fingers were remarkably similar to her own but tipped with curved black nails and in those hands it held to a silver length of which looked to be aluminum or something close in composition. Shaped like the barrel of a rifle, it stepped past the beast and moved beside her in silent strides as though aware of an impending danger lurking near.

And beyond the monster of black she looked into the origin of that emerald sun and felt her mind falling into her throat.

"Quiet, I think I see something moving up ahead."

Wilmont came to a sudden stop behind the sheriff. Standing with their backs pressed to the stone curvature of the wall, they kept away from the jade light knifing the darkness down the shaft.

"I don't see anything, sheriff."

"I saw it damnit—saw something just past that light."

Moving with the utmost secrecy, Caudel edged into the river of green light and peaked into a chamber, and his eyes rounded in his head when his pupils captured the image of Brittney, a ball of naked, pale limbs, coated in that lime gleam and caked by the caverns dust, her hands bound by black wire. But it was the monster that sat behind her, his aspect a black portal which the green light cut around. As to the source of the light, he could vaguely descry what looked to be a silver object of great width and height. *Big enough to enter this cave*, he thought.

Roughly shaped into that of a giant clam of silver, Caudel felt his limbs tighten and his body tremble and sweat break on his face.

It came from the stars, it came from the stars …

Leaning back into the shadow, unable to take another step, Caudel felt a pain in his chest, and his pulse quicken, and a vibratory prickling raced up his arm—

"*Sheriff!*"

What happened next was but a flash as two weapons came together in a burst of light that blinded the eyes.

Deputy Wilmont detached himself from the thin layer of shadow on the wall. He stepped into the green column and shouldered his rifle all in the space of two seconds.

And standing to his front a short distance down, was a similar shape, but taller and slightly more broad in width.

Wilmont screamed as his rifle thundered in the confines of the cave and in turn absorbed a bolt of cosmic color that streaked into his chest, atomizing his body into a shower of bloody particles that painted the walls black.

It was that quick.

Caudel stared down at the smoking, waxing lump of ankles that smoldered in flame inside the boots. Shivering, he held to the shadows, the shotgun shaking with his terror. There was no sound, and Caudel wondered if he were alone, and whatever it was that he briefly saw in that light, had now retreated further into the cave

It took him a moment to collect his air. He could not turn away from that smoking clot that was Wilmont. Pieces of him had embedded the walls, and Caudel was lucky to have avoided the spears of bone which impaled the rock around him. Blood was hot on his face, in his mouth, and flecked his uniform red, and spotted the shotgun and oiled his knuckles.

Minutes had passed and Caudel slowly recovered a strength that would allow him to proceed further into the cave, something which his mind had advised him against if he intended to live.

But Caudel felt the specter of death, and its grim cloak fell near as he moved further down into the cave, unimpeded.

Now entirely revealed in the green glow, Caudel kept low and sought the rounded block of a crumbling boulder. A suitable defense—at least he hoped.

Peaking around the side of the boulder, his face

limned green, he was able to clearly define shapes and structures and the outlines of two figures, one slim, and the other all too familiar.

But it was the other figure that held Caudel's glare. That purple skinned thing with the black oval eyes and slender silver tube in its arms. Immediately hit with a loathing that surpassed the blood and flesh monster of black, this fresh horror had conjured an almost atavistic dread. It was not human, nor entirely bestial, but something far worse; an invader; an interloper from beyond the known stars.

A goddamn alien; that's what it is, a goddamn alien.

A list of species original to this planet had failed to offer an cogent explanation for what now stood looming above Brittney. Curled as she was, Caudel could see her eyes huge and frightened looking on that purple body. And he could understand the fear and repulsion and aversion she must have felt being so near. It lowered itself down, brushed her face and she screamed a shrill whisper at the feel of its fingers searching her body. The beast stood immobile, only its broad shoulders and back heaving with air. Even its eyes were black, as if it were in slumber or seized by some enchantment.

It can't be ... it just can't be.

But it was real as the blood on his face and those boots behind him curdled in red slop and jutting ankle bone. It was as real as those children that lay smeared into raw puddles and had their skulls pounded into flat piles of meat. And for what reason? What purpose did it have? To simply rampage the land and break bodies and eat breathing things? There was no real motive behind any of it, and that thought alone was the most frightening thing. For if this thing was an alien and the beast perhaps its pet or beneath some spell, was their presence on this planet for some sort of hunting expedition? But what were they hunting for? And if not sport, perhaps the earth provided rudimentary experience or testing? The possibilities were endless and all so grim.

Confounded and perhaps at odds with his own mind, he did the only thing he thought himself capable of doing right then.

He came around the corner, eyes burning with hate and rage in his throat. Rage for all them broken bodies at the camp and his parter which lay splashed behind him. To all those that fell to its evil. He brought up the gun and fired a single shell that crashed into the alien thing.

It turned and responded with a terrible whistling hiss that shook Caudel's mind. But he racked that pump and fired off another shell, catching it in the chest. Spots of green liquid beaded down its body, and something that could have been a scream or command, revitalized the eyes of the beast which pierced the green of the cave with red and came charging at Caudel with an atrocious pealing scream in its mouth.

Working the slide, Caudel chambered another

shell just as the beast fell into him, knocking the sheriff from his boots, winging him further back into the cave.

Shaking himself, coughing out a lung of dust and blood, aware of the monster's vibrations beneath his back, Caudel brought up the gun just as the beast filled his eyes with its terrible bulk.

"GO BACK TO HELL WHERE YOU CAME FROM!"

The shotgun echoed loudly as the flame leaped from the barrel and the beast bellowed as its face absorbed the blast, wedging its skull down the center in a gushing fountain of black blood.

It staggered backward in a drunken stride, blood and gobbets of brain and strange black ink flooding its chest before it toppled and lay still in a spreading black clotted puddle.

Racking the slide, Caudel had no time to grin at the sudden demise of the beast.

Rising with great effort to his feet, he felt the air rip above him and a great beam of mystic color arced over his head and crashed into the wall with a brilliant splatting flame.

Rising the shotgun, Caudel held his fire.

Brittney, naked, shielded the violet coated alien. Her body pinned to its serpent scaled chest. Her legs kicked and her bound arms hammered at the thing, but it showed no pain or slowing of its feet which shuffled back to the silver object and its gaping green portal.

Realizing what it was intending to do, Caudel dashed forward, his eyes over the shotgun and screamed for Brittney to duck.

Her eyes held desperation and terror. In those eyes were pools of despair and hopelessness and dreams and life. Tears sheeted her face, and Caudel felt the pain back in his heart.

A short distance gapped them, and Caudel tossed aside his shotgun, ripped free his pistol and raced towards the green portal.

But a blinding flash sent him reeling to the ground in confusion. Covering his eyes, he blinked through the startling light and saw, screaming mutely in the portal, Brittney, her eyes rounded and her mouth wide, and the thing behind her a black blur as both were suddenly shut inside the craft.

"NO!"

Fighting to his feet, blood trickling from his lips and the pain in his heart increasing, Caudel fired at the silver craft and the bullets whistled and flattened against the hull.

Tossing his gun at the object, Caudel watched in stunned amazement as the craft levitated quietly from the cavern floor with no more sound than a mountain wind. Dust billowed and blinded Caudel with grit and layered over him in a talcum-like mist.

A sudden shaking of the mountain below him caused him to leap just as the craft burst in a scintillating shield of starlight and shot past him, down the shaft and out into the night like a dashing comet.

CHAPTER 21

On his way back up the mountain, a convoy of headlights strung out behind him, Rundell had one of the most horrifying and bizarre moments of his life—besides facing that hulking black mutant of fur and fangs. It was a woman, on the side of the road. Aside from being caked in blood and dust, she was dragging something behind her. Took but a moment for Rundell to see that it was a headless corpse, coated thick in road dust. After confronting her, he learned that her name was Julie, one of the counselors from the camp, and the body belonged to Angela, another counselor. She was taken by another vehicle back down the mountain for help, the body was placed in the bed of a pickup, covered over in a tarp.

It took a lot of convincing for Rundell to gather the people and reinforce the camp, even a bit of fabricating and outright lies.

He told the assembled that there was a bear hurting children up at the camp, and it was the same bear that had killed the Miller's earlier in the day, and butchered the hikers a year past. He told them all that the sheriff would reward the shooter with a sizable sum of cash for the body of the bear. And that fact alone earned a lot more attention, so Rundell had himself a small war party and they beat up that road fast, headed for the camp.

Once they had arrived, the reality hit them all in the face like a blast of arctic wind. Some people were standing around not saying much, others were instantly helping the survivors, of which there were very few.

Rundell explained to the men and women who volunteered their time, that there was something out in these woods and it was not even a little bit funny as to what that thing was. His case was helped that much better by some of the survivors who told of what they saw or what they thought it was. One of which was Jake, but he had neither the tongue nor the sanity to speak much about anything relating to the beast. Instead he just sat there on the ground, his knees in his chest, crying and looking on the lake.

But some of the more wide bellied types smelling of liquor were poking jokes at the ranger.

"Is it Bigfoot?" somebody asked, and that got some laughs.

But most folks weren't laughing or had the stomach to even speak. The smell of blood hung in the air and it got into your pores and up your nose and on your tongue. It was heartbreaking, and it was only by the dim light of the moon that most people were looking onto those dark masses rather than lighted piles of child bones and blood smeared around them in such volume that it would sicken the mind with detail. But once the sun crowned the ridge, all the horror would be revealed in color.

Rundell looked around and searched but still hadn't found Caudel or Wilmont—no sign of either.

He tried the radio but nothing was coming through except for static. Finally, after maybe an hour of cleaning through the place and people standing around in groups shouldering rifles and speaking in low tones, someone shouted.

"Hey, hold up right there!"

Rundell faced the voice.

"Ranger over here!"

Rundell hurried over. "What is it?"

"Saw something out there—in the trees."

Soon there were flashlights spotting the woods and there was a figure limping around behind the trees.

"What the hell is it?" someone asked.

But Rundell knew. "*Sheriff!*"

Rundell raced forward, and stopped just as Caudel emerged into the myriad beams.

There were gasps at the condition of the sheriff.

"Sheriff—what the hell happened, where's Wilmont?"

Caudel leaned against Rundell.

"Somebody help me out!"

A man ran forward, took an arm and hung it

over his shoulder.

They carried Caudel into an open space until he pushed them away, told them in this croaking voice to give him some room.

So they did.

He stood there, shaking and shivering as though ice filled his blood. Covered in a fine sheet of granule dust, he was mottled with blood and bits of red, meaty things. His eyes were black holes in a powdered white face, even his grin, which was starting to spread open his lips, looked like a black gash. It was a disturbing appearance, like something that just crawled out of a grave.

"Roy, what happened?" Rundell asked him in a timid voice.

Caudel looked at the ranger, that grin on his face getting too big; the powder on his face cracked apart like dried mud and laughter started choking up his throat, and the sound of it was poison to the ears.

Rundell wanted to say something but his mouth was drying up and he backed away with the others, frightened by that laughter and that face.

Caudel continued to laugh and that laughter seemed to fill the woods in a black wave that emulated it and pushed it back out over the camp in a maddening cackle that uncoiled the nerves.

Caudel pointed to the black abyss above him. "*It came from the stars! It came from the stars! It came from the stars!*"

The laughing grew and continued to grow to

terrifying inflection, even as the black woods around them came alive with a hundred burning red eyes.

Afterword

Hope you enjoyed this madness. OGRE was a fun piece to write. If you enjoy trash and classic horror films like myself, you probably noticed bits of Grizzly (1976), Don't Go In The Woods (1981), Just Before Dawn (1981), Abominable (2006), and Demonwarp (1988). Each of the above mentioned titles are some of my favorite woodland horror films. I plucked out pieces of each and shaped them into my own vision. I originally intended to have this centered around a group of kids at camp, but decided to make them exclusive fodder for the beast. I wanted to focus on the counselors, but again, I found myself gravitating towards new ideas as I wrote the piece—which generally happens with everything I write.

A little update:

I'm working on a new title—a new addition to the Slasherback Series—that I aim to have released by early August. I'm working hard on *Jungle Rot*, my military cosmic horror piece that centers around a group of soldiers in Vietnam, which is being published by *D&T Publishing*. I'm re-writing *The Pail,* a Halloween novella, and I will have that released before Halloween, sometime in October. I have two other projects that will close out the year, both holiday pieces. I have several other projects in the works and might even just release those too. We'll see how the world treats my mind.

Now that I got that out the way, if you turn to the next page, I have something special. A true account of mine. Something that happened to me as a boy during a camping trip. The memory is still in my head and I will do my utmost to deliver it in a way that gives it credit. I'll be telling this from a first person perspective, because that's how I remember it. I was around 7/8 years of age at the time, but the clarity has stuck with me into old age. So, if you feel up to it, turn the page and lets get this going.

Shasta Lake, CA
1988

It was dark. Not so dark where we couldn't see where our feet were carrying us, but that almost purple darkness that hangs in the woods just as the sun sinks below the ridge. I was with my mom's boyfriend at the time. I'll call him Steve. Well, Steve and I decided to do some night fishing. It was my first time and I thought it would be sort of cool to leave the campsite and go into the woods and fish. I liked fishing, always had, still do.

I remember us driving around these winding forest roads that were made all that more dark as the trees on either side were towering black walls. I can still see the shadows thickening in those woods as we drove on. We came out into a clearing, over a bridge, and I remember Steve slowing the truck down to get a look. Below us was a broad river hemmed by boulders and shrub and some flat clearings further out that looked awesome, and I wished we could have checked those spots out. Steve wanted to check it out too, but figured we better go somewhere a bit more easily accessible, so we drove on.

After a while we came across what looked like some sort of trail-path off the side of the road, and opened in front of it was a shoulder of gravel. If you looked closely you could catch glimpses of the lake sitting out there behind the pines. Steve said it looked good so we pulled in to the lot and parked. We weren't the only ones there I noticed, because there was a small yellow pickup parked beneath some low branches and I remember it having a bunch of fishing decals and flag stickers on the windows.

Once outside, we grabbed our gear from the back and headed off down the trail. And that's when the woods started getting real dark.

Steve guided us down the trail with a flashlight and all I could keep looking at were those woods that bracketed us on that narrow path. I kept thinking I saw something in those woods and remembered earlier a ranger coming to the campground and warning people about some bears spotted in the area, so I'm thinking there was something watching us and following us in there. I even remember hearing those particular snapping and cracking sounds you hear in the woods. Like a common kid in the woods, I'm thinking of things that couldn't possibly be real; monsters and all those big fanged varieties that take shape in young minds when out in the woods.

It was a short hike to the lake, nothing that ate up much time. Immediately, I look out over the lake and that lake was a black mirror. I mean it was *black*. And it was flat and I could see the sky reflected in it and the stars, even the moon. It was so wild to my mind at the time.

Steve looked around a bit and pointed to a finger of land that extended out into the lake a ways. Looked like a good spot to toss a line so we headed on over there.

Keeping close to the shore, I still remember my eyes locked on the woods as those trees became one thick belt of black.

There was a man on the shore fishing. He said something to Steve and then the both of them started talking about what sort of fish were in the lake and Steve asked if the man was having any luck. The man told him that he caught three and went on to pull this chain out of the water and there were three fat trout clamped to the end.

After we left the man behind, we walked out across that finger of land. With our gear readied, we cast out and waited for the first bite. But after a while, it was looking like nothing was biting. I remember looking at the sky and seeing bats crossing the moon and hearing their squeaking and squealing sounds. The gnats and mosquitoes were coming out and hovering over the lake in thick clouds.

The man that we ran into earlier cast out a final line and I can still see that bobber he was using. It was some sort of glow-in-the-dark piece that looked really cool floating on the surface of that black water. I watched him reel it back after a moment and he packed his gear and took off. I was thinking that man was crazy to walk into the woods with not even a flashlight to guide him.

Well, Steve and I were out there for about an hour when he decided we'd had enough and there was nothing biting but the gnats and mosquitoes. So we packed our gear and started back.

Now, this is the moment that the woods and the shore were just swallowed over by black. I mean, I remember it being so dark that I felt blind. If you've ever spent time in the woods at night, away from all those lights in the city, then you may have an idea just what the hell I'm talking about.

Steve popped the flashlight on and we walked up the shore, keeping away from the woods, which I was happy about. We'd gone maybe a quarter of the way up when something shuffled in the sand behind us.

It was me who heard it first and I turned around thinking I would see something. But after turning away from that flashlight beam all I could see was a solid wall of black. I could hear the lake lapping the shore, and could still hear the bats circling in the sky and some crickets doing their thing in the woods. I turned back to Steve and saw him up a ways and hurried after him.

After I caught up with him, I heard that sound again, but louder, and it was close. So this time I tell Steve; tell him I heard something behind us. He thought I was playing and told me as much. To reassure me—and maybe himself—he put the light behind us, but as was to be expected, was nothing there that we hadn't seen when we first got there.

We continued on and started talking about things the rest of the walk, unrelated things I can't recall, but before we hit the trail, something big thumped behind us. Like the sound of two heels smacking the ground. And that sound locked me up and even Steve turned around real quick and put his light out there, swinging its beam from the shore to the woods.

He gave this weird laugh in his throat when there was nothing there, but I felt like something was out there, just keeping away from the light. Anyway, we continued into the path and were now wedged between those forest walls, and that's when things got *real* scary.

About half way up, that same sound came up behind us again, and I shit you not, that it sounded like somebody heavy running up behind us and it was right fucking there—like right behind us, waiting for us to turn around and see it.

I remember my eyes opening real wide and I'm pretty sure that's the first time I actually felt *real* fear. Steve, too, I could see was a bit shaken and he stood there a moment and kept that light on the trail and spotted the woods with its beam, even swung it up in the trees.

"What the hell is that?" he asked, and his voice was barely above a whisper.

I had no breath in my lungs; I was too scared to say anything right then. I felt like dropping my gear and running.

"Let's hurry up," he said, and that's what I remember him saying.

We were almost to the truck when it sounded like something was just in the woods beside us; like right there and if we turned we would see it and I'm pretty sure that whatever it was would have had me screaming and running off into the road. That sound was the last straw for Steve. He swung his light into the woods and started shouting real loud. I can't remember what he said, but I remember his voice—he was scared, something I had never once believed he was capable of being.

There was a strange smell in the air, and something moved off quickly into the woods but we couldn't see it all that well. But I swear to you —the reader—that I saw something big and black in those woods. Was it a bear? I have no fucking clue. And honestly, to this day, I remember it being much taller than any bear I've ever seen in real life or in movies or in pictures.

I turned to look at Steve and I will always remember that face of his. It was the face of *terror*. I was young, remember, and I have never seen a face like that, besides on a few faces I've seen in horror movies I was able to rent back at the time.

Back in the truck, I remember the silence between us. I kept looking at Steve like he was going to say something, but he never did. He turned the radio on after a moment, probably trying to get out of his head, but that face—that face was still there and he never talked about that shit again. Never said shit to my mom. It was forgotten and never discussed.

It was my first—and not last—creepy experience in the woods …

Printed in Great Britain
by Amazon

15968918R00098